"Tyler will open the show with a brief description of what *Video High* is all about," Jeff Russell, the group's advisor, said. "Then he'll introduce Sharon. Sharon, by the way, have you had any responses to your survey?"

"Not yet," Sharon replied. "But I've got a good idea of what kind of answers I'll be getting. Kids *are* having sex. Some use condoms, some don't. I don't think they take it very seriously."

"Take what seriously?" Tyler asked. "Condoms or sex?"

"Both."

Zack broke in. "I don't think Sharon should talk about this survey on television."

"Why not?" Debra asked. "I thought we decided . . ."

"It'll make Greenwood look bad," Zack declared. "There are some subjects that shouldn't be talked about in public."

"Excuse me, Zack," Jeff said. "We've already decided on this topic for the first show. And I think the majority of us agree it's an important one. Now, Kris, do you have anything to report?"

"I've got my questions for the homecoming queen candidates all planned," Kris said.

"Fine," Jeff said. "Be sure to tell all four candidates we'll be taping at 2:00."

"I will," Kris replied. "But right now there are only three. Paula Skinner isn't a candidate anymore."

For the first time at that meeting, Jade spoke. "Why?"

Kris saw no reason not to tell the truth. "Paula Skinner's pregnant."

WHEN YOU HAVE GIRL FRIENDS —
YOU HAVE IT ALL!

Follow the trials, triumph, and awesome adventures of five special girls that have become fast friends in spite of — or because of their differences!

Janis Sandifer-Wayne,	a peace-loving, vegetarian veteran of protests and causes.
Stephanie Ling,	the hard-working oldest daughter of a single parent.
Natalie Bell,	Los Angeles refugee and street-smart child of an inter-racial marriage.
Cassandra Taylor,	Natalie's cousin and the sophisticated daughter of an upper-middle class African-American family.
Maria Torres,	a beautiful cheerleader who's the apple of her conservative parent's eye.

They're all juniors at Seven Pines High. And they're doing things their own way — together!

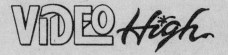

#1:MODERN LOVE

MARILYN KAYE

Z·FAVE
KENSINGTON PUBLISHING CORP.

Z-FAVE BOOKS are published by

Kensington Publishing Corp.
475 Park Avenue South
New York, NY 10016

Z-Fave and the Z-Fave logo are trademarks of Kensington Publishing Corp. (Scream and logo, the Nightmare Club and Logo, You -Solve-It-Mysteries, Time Benders)

First Printing: February, 1994

Printed in the United States of America

For Elise Donner:
editor, neighbor, and best of all, friend.

One

Heavy metal was *not* Sharon Delaney's favorite type of music. Still, there was nothing better for wrenching her eyes open, getting her out of bed, and into the shower. She returned to the bedroom a few moments later, her head wrapped in a towel. The radio was still blasting, and the deejay's voice was shrill.

"Good Monday morning, Atlanta! Rise and shine and greet the first official day of autumn! At 7:10 a.m., it's eighty-eight degrees in the shade and—"

With one hand, Sharon switched off the radio and with the other, she pulled the towel off her head. She dressed quickly, in her lightest weight pants and a t-shirt. Whipping a comb through her damp, light-brown hair, she mentally congratulated herself on her decision three weeks ago to have her hair cut short. It would dry by itself on the way to school.

Downstairs, in the kitchen, her parents and her kid brother were gathered at the table. "Morning," Sharon said as she grabbed the carton of orange juice from the counter and shook it. "There's more juice in the refrigerator," her mother told her.

"This is enough." Sharon started to raise the carton to her lips, and then caught her mother's look. She poured the juice into a glass and downed it in two big gulps.

"No breakfast?" her father inquired.

"No time," Sharon replied. "I've got a *News* meeting before class."

"You mean a 'Snooze' meeting," Kyle corrected her.

"Don't call it that," Sharon reprimanded the twelve-year-old.

"That's what *you* call it," he noted.

He had a point, and Sharon didn't have time to argue. "See y'all later," she said, blowing air kisses in their general direction. She snatched up her backpack and ran out the door.

It was like running into a steam bath. Having lived in Atlanta all her sixteen years, she was prepared for this feeling, but that didn't make the weather any more comfortable. The hot Georgia sun beat down on her relentlessly.

The first day of autumn. Hah! Why do they bother to give this time of year a name, she wondered. There was no difference between a Georgia August and a Georgia September. It was only a ten minute walk to Greenwood High School, but by the time she arrived, beads of perspiration were trickling down the side of her face.

Walking inside the old building, she sighed in

relief to discover that after almost three weeks of school, the air conditioning had finally started to work. Her footsteps echoed in the nearly empty hallway. She would have liked to stop in a restroom, to repair any damage caused by the humidity to her now dry hair. But she didn't want to be late for the meeting.

She needn't have worried. In the large office of the *Greenwood High Weekly News*, about a dozen kids were still milling around and talking. Passing through the group, she waved, smiled, and greeted friends, and then took a seat toward the back of the room. This was her second year on the staff of the *News*, and she knew the unwritten rule—only seniors sat up front. Juniors and other inferior types stayed in the back.

A meek-looking sophomore was passing out copies of the most recent *News*. Sharon took one, and examined the pages.

Her brother was right—the *News* was as good as a sleeping pill. Sharon fought the urge to yawn as she skimmed the reports on sporting events, the debate over dress—formal? casual?—for this year's Christmas dance, and the predictable editorial on cafeteria food. Toward the back of the paper, she found the piece she'd been assigned to write—an article on the Spanish Club's pot luck dinner, including a recipe for gazpacho soup. Not exactly the kind of story she had fantasized about writing when she'd joined the staff.

"Sharon, hi."

She turned to see a boy in baggy jeans and a

faded work-shirt standing by her. Soft, wavy brown hair fell to his shoulders.

"Tyler! What are you doing here?"

He slipped into the empty seat next to hers. "I've been thinking about joining the newspaper staff. Is it okay if I sit in on the meeting?"

"Sure, I guess so." She eyed him quizzically, and he shifted about in his seat.

"Why are you looking at me like that?"

"I'm just surprised to see you here," she said. "I didn't know you were interested in writing."

"Well, you were talking about the *News* Saturday night, and, I don't know, it sounded like . . . fun." His voice trailed off and he smiled uncertainly.

The memory of their first date brought a smile to her face. They'd talked about movies, politics, and the new English teacher they both admired. But as far as she could recall, her only comment about the *News* had been in the form of a complaint. His eyes strayed from hers, and he seemed almost embarrassed. It occurred to her that maybe he had come to the meeting to see *her*—or was that a wildly egotistical thought? They didn't exactly have a relationship, not after one date. But remembering that date gave her a nice, warm feeling, and she suspected maybe it did the same for him.

Suddenly, he looked directly into her eyes, gave her a crooked, abashed grin, and winked. It was like a silent confession that what she was thinking was true. Her own smile widened. And then they both faced forward as Terri Rosen, the editor, took her place at the front desk.

"Could I have everyone's attention, please?" Terri's normally placid face revealed a line of concern, and there was a tinge of anxiety in her voice. "Guys, we've got a problem. When I became editor of the *News* this year, I decided we would follow the same format as last year. Remember, we talked about this at the first meeting, and you all agreed with me?"

Not true, Sharon thought. *She'd* proposed a change or two. But no one had paid much attention.

"Anyway," Terri continued, "the other day, in the cafeteria, I heard some kids talking about the paper. And do you know what they called it? The 'Snooze'!"

Tyler glanced at Sharon and she knew immediately that he was having the same reaction to this comment as she was having. Surely this couldn't be the first time Terri had heard that old nickname for Greenwood's less-than-electrifying newspaper.

"Well, I took a good, long, hard look at the *News*," Terri went on. "And I have to admit, those kids were right. It's boring. And we've got to do something about it. The *News* is the voice of Greenwood High, and I don't think we're living up to our responsibility to the students."

Sharon sat up straighter. At last, someone other than herself wanted to turn this dreary paper around!

"I want ideas," Terri told them. "I want fresh,

11

new stories. I want to grab our readers by the throat and shake them up."

Sharon practically leaped to her feet. The editor appeared taken aback for a moment, then nodded in Sharon's direction.

"I'm so happy to hear you say this, Terri. I think the *News* should be dealing with important issues, the ones that affect us."

"Such as?"

Sharon dove into her backpack and pulled out the folder of clippings she'd cut out from the daily Atlanta newspapers. She became aware that Tyler was watching her with interest, and she experienced a mild fluttering in her stomach. Was she really about to bring up this subject in front of a guy she . . . well, liked?

Maybe she could get her point across without using words that would be embarrassing. She spoke carefully.

"I'm sure you've all heard about what's coming up at the school board meeting this week. I think we need to address this issue."

She paused, expecting a reaction from the group—enthusiasm, shock, anger, *something*. But as she gazed around, she realized they didn't know what she was getting at.

"Come on, you know what I'm talking about. It's been in all the papers, and on the TV news. The big controversy . . . ?"

Still, there was no response. She was going to have to spell it out for them. "Everyone's worried about the spread of AIDS among teenagers, and they're arguing about whether or not the high schools should distribute condoms. Free. To students."

That got a reaction. Sharon kept her eyes on Terri, but she heard a sharp intake of breath, a whisper, some chairs scraping the floor as kids turned to look at her. At least there were no giggles. That was encouraging.

But Terri's next words weren't. "I don't think we want to get into a subject like that, Sharon."

"Why not?"

"It's a school board decision. It's got nothing to do with us."

"It's got *everything* to do with us!" Sharon exclaimed. "We're the ones who would be using the condoms!"

Big mistake. A titter went through the room. Trying to be a good sport, Sharon forced a feeble smile. "Come on, you know what I mean."

Terri shook her head. "This is a touchy subject, Sharon. Like you just said yourself, it's a controversy."

"But I could write about it objectively," Sharon argued. "I'd show both sides."

"It wouldn't matter," Terri said. "Mr. Quimby would have a fit."

Sharon stared at her in bewilderment. "What does the assistant principal have to do with this?"

Terri replied patiently. "Sharon, you know that Mr. Quimby determines the budgets for school activities. And Mr. Quimby doesn't like controversy. We've got a great budget this year, and I don't want to do anything that might turn him off. Now, does anyone else have any ideas about livening up the paper?"

Sharon sank back into her chair. From the corner of her eye, she caught a glimpse of Tyler, looking at her oddly. She couldn't tell if he was shocked, or amused, or sympathetic.

"Come on, you guys," Terri urged. "Give me some ideas."

"We could have a horoscope in each issue," someone suggested.

Terri brightened. "That's not bad."

"How about a gossip column?" another staff member called out. "You know, like who broke up with who, who was seen with who, that sort of thing."

"I love it!" Terri exclaimed.

Sharon closed her eyes. She couldn't say she was devastated by this, or even surprised. But she'd had hopes for the *News* this year, and Terri's earlier words had kindled them. Now, those hopes were completely extinguished.

"Nice try," Tyler whispered to her. She turned to him. Was it possible that he was actually a little impressed by her efforts? That helped lift her spirits . . . a little.

Now the room was buzzing with excited chatter about horoscopes and gossip columns and cartoons. Then Terri began assigning writers to feature stories, and what had been dreary became downright depressing.

"Pete, I want a story on the outlook for this year's basketball team. Amy, could you do a review of the new cheerleading routines? Great.

Now, what do you guys think? Is it, too soon to print the questionnaire on prom themes?"

It was all Sharon could do to keep from screaming. Basketball. Prom themes. Didn't anyone care about *real* issues?

"We'll also need more interviews with the new teachers," Terri continued. She checked a list. "Let's see, there's Ms. Paulo, the new librarian, and Mr. Russell in English . . ."

Sharon's hand shot up. "I'll do the interview with Mr. Russell."

"Thanks, Sharon," Terri said sweetly, "but you did such a nice job on the Spanish Club dinner, I've assigned you to write a report on the French Club dinner."

Sharon pressed her lips together tightly. She knew what was going on. Terri was punishing her for having the gall to propose a controversial article, and for being foolish enough to think that she, a mere junior, could write a major story.

Why did she even bother? The *Greenwood News* was utterly, totally hopeless.

Finally, the meeting was over. Tyler walked out with her. "French Club dinner, huh? Doesn't sound too exciting," he commented.

"It won't be," Sharon said glumly. "It'll be boring. Which means it's perfect for the Snooze."

"Why do you stay on the staff if it's so boring?" Tyler asked.

"I don't know. I guess I keep hoping I can make some changes." She could hear her voice rising, becoming more animated, and she didn't bother to try to keep it under control. "There's

15

so much going on in the world, right here in this school even, so much we should be thinking about. But we just look the other way and worry about . . . prom themes."

"And you're not going to give up?"

"Not unless I find something better." She glanced at him furtively to see how he was taking this. Some guys were put off by her determination. She was pleased to see that Tyler didn't look the least bit turned off by her passionate declaration.

It was eight o'clock now, and the halls were crowded with students on their way to homerooms. The air was filled with the sounds of Monday morning greetings and lockers slamming. So when Tyler asked her something in a low tone, she couldn't hear him.

"What did you say?"

She was surprised to see a light flush come into his face. He raised his voice slightly. "You want to get together after school?"

"Today?"

He nodded.

"I can't," she said, hoping he'd hear the sincere regret in her words. "I've got to go to a student council committee meeting."

"You're involved in *that*, too?"

"I'm supposed to write it up for the *News*." She made a face, to make clear that she'd rather be doing anything *but*.

"Oh. Well, what about this weekend. Saturday night?"

"I'd like that . . ." she began carefully.

16

"Great!"

"But there's a chance my family's going down to Savannah to see my grandmother. Can I let you know later this week?"

"Yeah, okay, sure."

"By Wednesday," she promised him. They separated. She gazed after him for a moment, and hoped she hadn't discouraged him. It was hard to tell. She didn't know Tyler well at all. He was a senior, so they'd never had a class together. She would see him in the cafeteria, with other seniors, but even in a crowd he'd always struck her as something of a loner—not unfriendly, but not into school programs or sports or any big group activities.

Two weeks ago, they'd run into each other at a book store near Emory University. They'd started talking, and discovered they both had Mr. Russell for English. She'd been impressed with the way he had openly admired a teacher, when the cool thing to do was to ridicule them. When they parted, he'd asked her out. She'd been surprised—but pleased.

Still, even after their date, he was something of a mystery. Oh, she had some idea as to his opinions about movies and politics and books, but he never revealed anything personal, about his own interests, or hobbies, or goals. She didn't really know him at all—but she was beginning to think she'd like to. She actually found herself smiling on the way to the classroom. But when she arrived, and saw the stack of untouched

17

newspapers resting by the door, her irritation returned.

She plunked herself down at her desk, next to Debra's, her best friend, who was oblivious to her arrival. As usual, Debra's head was bent over a book. Sharon had to let out a major, heartfelt groan to get her attention.

Debra glanced up, read Sharon's expression, and slammed her book shut. She swung her legs around to the side and faced her. "Okay, what's wrong?"

"*News* meeting."

There was no real need for her to say more. Debra had heard her complaints weekly for over a year. But Sharon went on anyway. "I proposed a feature article on the condom controversy. And guess what that wimp Terri Rosen said?"

"Too controversial," Debra replied immediately.

"Exactly." Sharon put her elbow on her desk and rested her chin in her hand. "I don't know why I bother. It's always the same."

"Then stop banging your head against a brick wall," Debra said matter-of-factly. "Quit. You spend all your free time writing articles you don't even want to write. It's a waste! You're always saying you don't have time to study. Or shop, or go to a movie once in a while, or a museum. Or have a relationship."

Sharon didn't bother to argue. Debra wouldn't understand; she wasn't into extracurricular activities. She didn't belong to any clubs. She was probably the only black student at Greenwood who wasn't even a member of the African American Students League.

But Debra's last suggestion reminded her of other news. "Tyler was there. At the *News* meeting."

Now Debra actually showed some interest. "Oh, yeah?"

"He *said* he wanted to join the staff." Sharon grinned. "I don't mean to sound conceited, but I had a feeling that really wasn't what he was interested in."

Debra grinned back. Then she blinked. "Wait a minute. You talked about condoms with Tyler sitting right there?"

"Sure, why not?"

Debra shrugged. "You might be giving him some ideas."

"Oh, *please.*" Any further discussion was cut off with the arrival of the teacher and the ringing of the bell. This was immediately followed by the crackling of the intercom.

"May I have your attention for the morning announcements?" a hollow voice inquired.

As usual, half the class responded with a long, drawn-out "noooo."

The voice proceeded anyway, with the usual dull litany of club meetings, drama club auditions, sports practice sessions, and a plea for the return of overdue library books. Sharon tapped her pencil on the desk and tuned out the voice.

But with the final announcement, her tapping ceased.

"We are pleased to announce that Greenwood

High has been given a grant to begin its own city-wide cable television program. Students interested in participating are invited to sign up in the assistant principal's office."

With another crackle, the intercom went silent. Sharon made a note on her notebook cover, leaned back in her chair, and smiled thoughtfully.

"What are you looking so happy about?" Debra asked.

"I'm just thinking that I might take your advice," Sharon replied.

"Advice about what?"

"Quitting the *News.*"

Debra's eyes widened. "Really? That's great!" Then her eyes lit on the memo Sharon had just scrawled to herself: 'Cable TV show. Sign-up at Quimby's office.'

"Oh, Sharon," Debra groaned.

"What do you think?" Sharon asked eagerly.

Debra shook her head in resignation. "Out of the frying pan, into the fire."

Two

Debra folded her arms across her chest and fixed steely eyes on Sharon. "No."

"Oh, c'mon, it'll be fun," Sharon urged. "Think about it, Deb. Our own TV show!"

"But I don't *want* my own TV show," Debra stated. She glanced at their homeroom teacher and wished she would order the class to be quiet. Unfortunately, she never cared if the students talked, as long as they kept the noise down to a dull roar.

Resigned, she allowed Sharon to continue. She knew her friend wasn't going to give up easily.

"This is our chance to do something really interesting."

"How do you know it will be interesting?" Debra countered. "This TV show, it could be just as dull as the *News*. It could be just as trivial and boring as every other activity in this school."

"But we'll never know unless we get involved," Sharon argued.

"You can get involved," Debra said. "It's not for

me. You know how I feel about extracurricular activities. They're a waste of time. Sometimes I think these organizations just exist so the members have an excuse to throw a party every semester."

As usual, Sharon ignored her protest. "And we'd be working together! You were just saying the other day how we hardly ever have time to hang out together anymore. Between your manic study habits and my running around for the stupid Snooze—"

In a feeble attempt to change the subject, Debra interrupted. "Hey, did you read that short story Mr. Russell assigned? It's fantastic. You know, he's the best teacher I've ever had. I've never been crazy about literature, but—"

"Yeah, yeah, he's great," Sharon said. "Deb, why won't you even consider this thing?"

Debra shook her head wearily. For the zillionth time, she explained. "Sharon, you know I want to be a doctor someday. I want to get into the best possible university, I want early admission, and I need a scholarship. This means I have to make all As, I have to do brilliantly on the SATs, and—"

"And you need extracurricular activities," Sharon finished triumphantly. "I've seen those university applications. There's a great, big, fat space where you're supposed to list all your extracurricular activities. What are you going to put in that space, Debra?"

Debra was spared having to answer by the bell. The girls rose and moved out into the hall.

There, despite the noise, Sharon continued her lecture. "Universities want well-rounded students. You have to show them you have interests beyond academic stuff."

"I have lots of interests," Debra replied indignantly. "I read, I paint, I take violin lessons . . . you know that."

"I know that. But those universities don't."

Debra grimaced. She couldn't argue anymore, because she knew Sharon was right. Universities did like extra-curricular activities. But there never seemed to be enough hours in the day to do all the things she *wanted* to do, all the solitary activities she loved. It wasn't that she didn't like people—she just wasn't into working on projects that seemed trivial. And in her opinion, the activities at Greenwood were just an excuse for socializing. That was something Sharon just couldn't accept—that Debra wasn't into socializing like she was.

They were nearing the assistant principal's office, which they both had to pass to get to their next classes. "Okay, maybe I do need something extracurricular to put on my applications," Debra said. "But there's no reason why it has to be *this* activity. How about if *I* decide what's right for me?"

Sharon was silent for a moment. Then she gave Debra an abashed look. "Yeah, okay. I'm being pushy again, right?"

Debra grinned. "Right."

They were about to separate at the office door when Debra saw Mr. Russell coming out. The young, boyish English teacher looked vaguely disgruntled, but he greeted the girls with an easy smile. "You two interested in television?" he asked hopefully.

"I am," Sharon declared. "I was just about to sign up."

"Good," Mr. Russell said. "You'll be the first. I thought kids would storm this office to sign up." He scratched his head. "I don't get it."

Debra offered an explanation. "Greenwood High is pretty apathetic."

"I've noticed that," the teacher murmured. "Things were different when I was your age."

Sharon gazed at him in open admiration. "You guys were real radicals, right?"

He laughed. "I wouldn't call us radicals. But it's true, we wanted to change the world. Or at least, *talk* about it." He shook his head. "I'm really disappointed. There are so many issues and ideas we could deal with on this TV show. And I'm not just talking about politics or world problems. We could deal with personal stuff. Feelings. Relationships. Whatever you guys are thinking about."

Debra cocked her head to one side. "Sex, drugs, and rock and roll?"

"If you want," he replied. "*Students* are going to run this show. But if we don't get at least half a dozen kids signed up, it isn't going to fly."

"We?" Debra inquired.

"I'm the advisor." He glanced up at the clock. "I've got to get to my classroom. Glad you're interested, Sharon. What about you, Debra? Are you going to sign up?"

Sharon opened her mouth to respond, but Debra beat her to it. "Actually, I think I will." And she grinned as Sharon's mouth remained open in surprise.

From the other end of the hall, Tyler watched Sharon and her friend Debra talking to the new English teacher. Whatever they were talking about, Sharon looked excited. Her face was alive with enthusiasm. It was the expression that had first attracted him to her.

Other girls he'd gone out with tried hard to look like nothing in the world could excite them. They seemed to think it was totally uncool to show any emotions. Sharon . . . Sharon was different. She didn't care about being cool. That morning, at the *News* meeting, he'd been so impressed with the way she expressed herself, knowing she might be shot down by that snotty editor. She was even able to talk about condoms without blushing!

He thought back to their last date, Saturday night. They'd gone to a movie, which he had liked and she didn't. Some girls he knew would always agree with the guy. Sharon expressed her opinion freely. And at the same time, she listened to *his* opinion of the movie, and didn't mock him. He had a feeling he'd be able to share his private feelings with her, when he got to know her better. He wanted to tell her about the things that were important to him—his music, the songs he'd written, the way he could sit alone in his room for hours with his guitar. She seemed like the kind of person who would understand his dream—to form a band, not a typical run-of-the-mill rock band, but a band with a unique sound, that played music with words that had meaning, that *said* something. He never talked about this with his buddies, the guys he hung out with out of habit. Or with the girls he occasionally took out. He didn't think they'd understand how serious he was.

But Sharon might. She wasn't like those giggly, flirty girls. And she wasn't always fussing with herself. In the car, she didn't keep looking in the rearview mirror to check her face. She wasn't constantly applying lipstick or combing her hair. She was natural and *real*.

He'd only gone to the *News* meeting that morning to see her. He wasn't into writing news, only poems, songs. He didn't really want to join the staff, but he would if it meant he could spend more time with her. His eyes followed her as she and her friend went into Mr. Quimby's office.

"Hey man, what's up?"

He turned. "Hi, Gary."

His classmate grinned wickedly and waggled his eyebrows. "I saw you checking out that babe. What's the deal? You making it with her"

Tyler imagined what would happen to anyone who called Sharon a babe to her face. "No," he said shortly. "And her name's Sharon!'

He walked down the hall and went into the

26

office, but she must have left when his back was turned.

"You want to sign up?" the secretary asked in a bored voice.

"Sign up for what?" Tyler asked.

"That TV show thing. Mr. Russell told me to ask any student who came in." She indicated a sheet of paper. There were only two names on it. The first was Sharon's.

Tyler recalled the announcement in homeroom. This had to be more interesting than the Snooze, he decided. And if Sharon was involved. . . . "Yeah. I'll sign up."

He hurried out to get to his class on time. But as he passed the main entrance, he noticed a girl who seemed to be having a problem pulling the door open to get in. He held the door for her, and she limped in on crutches. He recognized her as a cheerleader, but he didn't know her name. "What happened to you?"

The pretty, fair haired girl gazed up at him mournfully. "It happened at cheerleading practice this morning. I was doing a triple back flip and I landed wrong."

"Did you break something?"

"Actually, it's just a sprain." A tear trickled down her face.

"Are you in pain?" Tyler asked sympathetically.

"No . . . but I'm—I'm off the squad for the whole season."

Tyler stood there awkwardly as she brushed

away the tear. "Oh. Gee, that's too bad. You need any help?"

"No, thank you," she said bravely. She hobbled off in the direction of the assistant principal's office.

Poor kid, Tyler thought. The bell rang, and as he ran down the hall, his thoughts returned to Sharon. *That* was a girl who wouldn't cry over a sprained ankle. *Or* cheerleading.

Kris gazed after the boy who'd held the door for her. He wasn't an athlete or a class officer, so she didn't know his name. She could tell he couldn't understand why she was so upset. Well, she couldn't expect anyone, not even another cheerleader, to understand. No one knew how much cheerleading meant to her, and why. No one had any idea how hard she'd worked, how much she'd overcome, to get this far.

From her first day at Greenwood last year, she'd struggled to be accepted, to become one of the popular girls. She'd joined the right clubs and kissed up to all the right people. She'd scrimped and saved, skipping lunches and cleaning a neighbor's house, so that she could have the right clothes. She dated the right guys, if only briefly. She couldn't let any guys, or any girls for that matter, get too close. They'd start wondering why she never invited them to her home.

Home . . . her lip curled in distaste at the word. Her so-called home was a dirty, battered cottage on one of the only run-down streets in the area. But nobody here would know that, not if she could help it. She explained her reluctance to bring people home by telling everyone her mother was an invalid. It wasn't exactly a lie. If alcoholism was a disease, her mother was definitely sick.

Once, back in the sixth grade, she'd been invited to a classmate's birthday party. There, she'd overheard the classmate's mother talking to another mother, and referring to Kris as 'trash.' Looking back, she couldn't blame the woman. Wearing a dress that didn't fit, with her unkempt hair and unwashed body, Kris must have looked like a child of the slums.

Well, those days were long gone. Nobody would call her trash here. Before starting high school, she'd given herself a cold, hard examination to determine how best to change her image. She knew she wasn't a genius, so she could forget about standing out academically. She wasn't creative, and she had no talents, so that ruled out areas like drama or singing. But she was pretty, more than pretty, and if she wasn't a great brain she was still smart enough to imitate others. And so she did. And when she was chosen as a cheerleader last year, she knew her efforts had paid off. Cheerleaders were celebrities. They were envied, and admired. She, Kris Hogan, was a *somebody*.

But that was yesterday. Today, she was a former cheerleader with a sprained ankle.

Well, there was one benefit to spraining an ankle, she decided as she limped toward Mr.

Quimby's office. You certainly got a lot of attention.

"Kris! What happened?"

"You poor thing!"

"Do you need any help?"

It took her ages to travel the distance to the office, and not because of the crutches. With each step, someone approached and she had to tell her story again and again.

In the assistant principal's office, she paused to look at a poster on the wall. 'Support the Greenwood Tigers' it demanded. Above the words was an enlarged photo of a typical Friday evening in the Greenwood High stadium. Guys in uniforms and helmets were on the field. A blurry crowd filled the stands. And before them were the cheerleaders, looking adorable in their short white skirts, their arms holding up big blue pom poms.

Kris could almost hear the cheering, she could feel the sense of power as she brought an entire stadium full of spectators to their feet, all their eyes on her . . . . Okay, maybe some eyes were on the game. Still, it was unbearably painful to accept the fact that it was all over for her. From now on, she'd be just another ordinary Greenwood student, nobody special.

"Shouldn't you be in class, young lady?" demanded an authoritative voice.

In an attempt to shift around to face the speaker, Kris caught her good foot in a crutch. Mr. Quimby clutched her arm and managed to prevent her from tripping.

"Are you all right?" he asked anxiously.

"Yes, I'm fine," she replied.

"Good," he said in relief. He turned to the secretary. "You're a witness, she said she's fine. I don't want any lawsuits."

Kris looked at him in bewilderment. She had no idea what he was talking about.

"Now, what are you doing in here?" Mr. Quimby inquired in a slightly more gentle tone.

"I have a note from the doctor, explaining why I'm late. I hurt my ankle this morning at cheerleading practice."

Quimby gasped. "On school grounds?"

"Don't worry," the secretary piped up. "All students involved in sports have to sign a release. We can't be held legally responsible."

Kris's eyes darted back and forth between them. Here she was, on crutches, her high school career ruined, and all they could talk about was lawsuits and legal stuff! She was so angry, fresh tears poured forth.

"Now what's your problem?" Quimby asked in alarm.

"I can't be a cheerleader anymore," she wept.

The assistant principal didn't appear to be the least bit concerned. "There are plenty of other activities you can join."

Now that she'd let the tears out, she couldn't stop them. "There's nothing as important as being a cheerleader."

"Of course there is," Quimby growled.

"Like what?"

31

"Well, there's the Glee Club, and the drama club . . ."

Kris shook her head.

"And there's this new TV show."

"What TV show?"

Quimby explained. "Greenwood has received a grant for students to create their own cable TV show." He made a 'humph' sound. "Personally, I think it's all nonsense. No one wants to watch a bunch of teenagers on television."

He went on in this vein, but Kris had stopped listening. Maybe she wouldn't have to be just an ordinary Greenwood student after all. Television . . . yes! It had definite possibilities. Suddenly, she could see herself, interviewing celebrities, modeling the new fall fashions . . . hundreds of thousands of people tuning in to see her. Why, a whole new career might be opening up for her!

Quimby directed her to the sign-up sheet, where she wrote 'Kris Hogan' with a flourish. It looked like a celebrity autograph. That struck her as a good omen.

She hobbled out of the office. Everyone was in class now, so the hall was empty, with the exception of some girl Kris didn't know. She was leaning against the wall next to the guidance counselor's office.

Kris eyed her curiously. She certainly didn't look like a typical Greenwood student. Her spiked, jet-black hair had a green streak in it. She wore a black t-shirt with a rip in one sleeve, tight black jeans with more rips, and black, evil-looking boots that laced up. On closer inspection, Kris noted with a shudder that the girl's nose was pierced. And when the girl turned her head, Kris's mouth fell open. One side of her head was shaved! Somebody should tell this kid that punk was *not* the style at Greenwood.

"What are you staring at?"

Kris was momentarily taken aback. Then, thinking that this could be one of her future viewers, she smiled brightly. "Hi! I'm Kris Hogan. Are you new here?"

The girl shoved her hands into her jeans pockets. "Why do you want to know?"

"Well, I was just curious . . ."

"Don't be," she snarled.

"Excuse me for asking," Kris replied. What a weird girl, she thought as she moved on. She shouldn't have bothered wasting any charm on *her*.

Jade sneered at the back of the prissy-looking blonde on crutches. Phony bitch, she thought. Acting like she cared who Jade was or where she came from. She was just like all the rest here. A bunch of phony, preppy, mindless morons, jocks, and bimbos. That's what she was locked up in this factory with. She'd made that judgment on the first day of school. Three weeks later, her opinion hadn't changed.

The guidance counselor's door opened. "Jade Barrow? Come on in."

Jade shuffled into the office and slumped

down into a chair. She had met this woman once before, but she couldn't remember her name. Luckily, there was a nameplate on her desk, which identified her as Ms. Klein. Not that Jade cared what her name was.

"How do you like Greenwood so far, Jade?"

"Oh, it's just fabulous," Jade replied, her voice dripping with sarcasm.

Ms. Klein looked at her sharply. "Are you getting to know many students?"

"No."

"Why not?"

"Because I haven't seen any I want to meet."

Ms. Klein studied her thoughtfully. "That's not a very good attitude, Jade. You'll never feel comfortable here unless—"

Jade broke in rudely. "Who says I want to feel comfortable? It wasn't my idea to come here."

"I realize that," the counselor said. "But you were having a lot of problems at your old school. Your grades were down. You were running with a disreputable gang." She paused, and then spoke carefully. "There was some concern that you were getting involved with drugs."

Jade shrugged. No response seemed to be necessary. Everything the counselor said was true.

Ms. Klein continued. "Your parents thought a change of environment might be helpful. And as I recall, you agreed with that."

That was true, too, but Jade wasn't about to confirm it. She was beginning to have regrets about that decision.

The counselor's voice was gentle. "Jade, I

know change is difficult. It takes effort and determination on your part. Most importantly, you have to want to change. Do you?"

She wasn't in the mood to argue. "Yeah. I guess."

Ms. Klein seemed doubtful, but she nodded. "Good. Then let's see how we can get you involved here at Greenwood. We have a fine program of extracurricular activities."

Jade uttered a short laugh. "Think I should join the Pep Club?"

"I think we can find something more in keeping with your interests. Let's see . . . are you interested in art?"

Jade shook her head.

"Science? Computers?"

"No."

"Well, there's this new cable television program we're creating. I was talking to Mr. Russell, the advisor, this morning. It sounds like it's going to be very contemporary, very . . . what's the word you kids use? Hip?"

Jade made a face. But at this point, she'd agree to anything to get this woman off her back. "Yeah, okay."

Ms. Klein smiled. "That's fine." She rose, and so did Jade. "Let's get you signed up right now." She escorted Jade out of the office and across the hall. "You know, Jade, I have a feeling that once you get involved and start making friends, you'll find Greenwood a very pleasant place to be."

Jade felt like a prisoner accompanied by a

guard. Ms. Klein actually waited to make sure Jade really signed the list.

"I'm glad we had this talk, Jade. And always feel free to drop by my office for a chat."

"Right," Jade mumbled, *That'll be the day,* she thought.

She looked at the other names on the list. She didn't know any of them. And she didn't have any particular desire to, either.

She became aware of voices coming from behind the closed door leading to the inner office. She recognized that old creep Quimby's high-pitched voice.

"Zack, there's nothing we can do about this."

The next voice was unfamiliar. "You can order a recount of the ballots. Mr. Quimby, student body president is too important a position to be held by an incompetent."

Jade had no desire to hear more. Student body president, she thought as she left the office. These jerks took the dumbest things so seriously.

Zack Stevenson was getting frustrated. For three years, he'd cultivated a cozy relationship with the assistant principal. He knew that Quimby thought he was an outstanding student. But this time, he wasn't getting through.

"Look, Mr. Quimby, you know as well as I do that I am the most qualified candidate for the office. You know my record."

"Yes, indeed I do," Mr. Quimby replied. "You've always demonstrated leadership qualities. And I'll admit, I was hoping you would be elected student body president. But the students seemed to have had other ideas." He shook his head sorrowfully. "They're not always the best judge of character."

"Exactly," Zack said with approval. "Then, for their own good, you could simply declare that there was an error in the counting of ballots."

"I can't do that, Zack. Much as you deserve the position, there are rules. Students elect their own officers. Can you imagine what would happen if the superintendent of schools learned that an assistant principal had falsified election results?"

The fear in Quimby's eyes told Zack that there was no way he'd ever convince the assistant principal to do it. He gave up. "Well, thank you for listening, Mr. Quimby."

He left the room. *Now* what, he wondered. He'd been so certain that he'd win that election. He'd been president of the sophomore class and president of the junior class. He hadn't run for senior class president because he'd wanted more, he'd wanted the top spot, student body president.

Losing the election had been a shock, a massive blow to his ego. But the worst part was reporting the news to his father. He could still see the disappointment and the disapproval in his father's face. State Senator Robert Stevenson's son was a failure.

He'd seen that look before. As a B student and a mediocre athlete, he hadn't been able to live up to his father's expectations in those areas. But still, his father had hopes for him. 'All you've got is good looks and charm, boy,' his father always told him. 'Use them!' Zack had listened. He always took his father's advice. It was his father who told him never to get too close to anyone, male or female. "Familiarity breeds contempt," he roared. "You want people looking up to you." As for girls, "Find someone pretty who doesn't make a lot of noise and looks good on your arm."

Up until now, the advice had paid off. But he had lost the election. The girl he'd taken out a few times this summer wouldn't even look at him now. He still sat with the same guys at lunch, the ones who led the most important activities and ran the school, but they barely acknowledged his presence.

At least the vote had been close. But that didn't change anything. Here he was, at the beginning of his senior year, with no power at all.

And nowhere to get any. Every other organization at school had established leaders. He couldn't join something and just be an ordinary member, not according to his father. "Don't be a sheep, boy," he'd bellow. "Don't *take* orders, *give* them! If you can't be a leader, you might as well be a bum."

A bum. That's what his father would be calling him now.

"You want to sign up?" the secretary asked.

"Sign up for what?" Zack asked.

She indicated the sheet on the desk. "I'm supposed to push this at any student who comes in. They need people to work on this TV show."

Zack recalled the announcement in homeroom. He hadn't paid much attention at the time, but now he started thinking. Television . . . the most powerful medium of all time. Presidents were chosen because of the way they came across on TV. News was only considered to be news if it was reported on TV. A person could use television to his advantage, if he had control of it.

He checked out the other names on the list. Jade Barrow, never heard of her. Kris Hogan, cute but dumb. Tyler Ratcliff, nice guy, easygoing—in other words, a pushover. Debra Lewis . . . he had a vague recollection of a black girl who kept pretty much to herself. Sharon Delaney . . . he knew who she was, but not much else. In any case, she was a girl, and he could handle girls.

And the advisor was Russell, the new guy in English. Quimby probably foisted this on him because he was too new to complain. Russell would be more than happy to have someone else around who knew the score. Someone to organize, to direct. Someone to take over. Someone a father could be proud of.

Zack scrawled his name on the list.

Three

Wednesday afternoon, Sharon waited outside Debra's last class, tapping her foot impatiently. Through the glass window in the door, she watched Debra engage in conversation with the biology teacher. As the hallway gradually emptied of students, she looked at the clock. "Hurry up, Deb," she muttered.

Finally, Debra emerged. "Come on," Sharon urged. "We don't want to be late."

Debra didn't exhibit any concern. "Meetings never start on time around here."

"How would you know?" Sharon countered. "You never go to any." She glanced at her friend curiously. "You still haven't told me why you changed your mind about signing up for this TV show."

"It was Mr. Russell," Debra replied. "I have a feeling that with him in charge, this might be something really worthwhile. But I warn you, if this turns out to be a typical Greenwood High waste-of-time activity, I'm dropping out."

"Okay," Sharon agreed. "But it won't be a waste of time. Not if *I* have anything to say about it. I just hope seniors won't try to take it over, so—'

"So you can?" Debra inquired. Then she bit her lip. Sharon could tell that Debra wanted to say more, but she was holding back.

"Spill it," Sharon demanded.

"Well, don't take this the wrong way, okay? But maybe you shouldn't make too much noise at this first meeting. You don't want to come across as too, too . . ." She was struggling for a word.

"Aggressive?" Sharon suggested.

Debra hesitated. "Yeah. Pushy."

Sharon took the criticism cheerfully. "I know, it's my worst habit. I guess I just get so excited sometimes, I don't realize how I sound to other people. Do me a favor, okay? If I talk too much at this meeting, kick me."

"With pleasure," Debra replied.

Sharon grinned. "But try not to leave a bruise."

They turned a corner and entered the older part of the building. "I forgot," Debra said. "Where is this meeting?"

"In the old chemistry lab, the one they've been using for storage." Sharon quickened her pace. "We better hurry. I want a good seat, and I know it's going to be packed."

She was wrong. The cavernous old lab was occupied by only two other students. And Sharon was more than a little surprised to see who those students were.

But she tried not to let her feelings show as

41

she greeted them. "Hi Kris, Zack." Kris smiled and waggled her fingers, while Zack nodded.

Sharon couldn't honestly say she knew either of them all that well, only by reputation. Zack was the son of a state senator, the most conservative senator in Georgia. Sharon had often heard her parents complain about Senator Stevenson's racist, sexist, totally antiquated attitudes. She knew she shouldn't hold his father's reputation against Zack, but she couldn't help but wonder if he shared his father's beliefs. She'd had one encounter with him, when he was running for student body president, and he'd oozed charm and arrogance.

Kris was a junior, like her, but they'd never run around together. She was one of those pretty, flirty girls, a popular cheerleader, who seemed to drift through high school without a care in the world or a thought in her head. Neither of them struck her as people she particularly wanted to work with.

Debra was oblivious to Sharon's concern. As uninvolved at school as she was, she wasn't aware of people's reputations. She nodded at the others and sat down. Sharon sat next to her, and smiled at Zack and Kris. She felt like she had to make some sort of effort, if they were all going to be working together. "I'm surprised there aren't more people here."

"I'm not," Zack stated. "Something like this requires commitment and an ability to think big. Not too many people have that kind of attitude."

His smile took them all in. "Personally, I'd rather work with a small, dedicated group."

His eyes were just too earnest, Sharon thought. He sounded like he was still running for something. But she had to admit, the guy had a certain style. Already, he'd managed to assert himself, and flatter them at the same time.

Debra, who never wasted a minute, had her head deep in a book. Kris, too had found a way to occupy the time. With a little mirror perched on her lap, she was carefully applying mascara. Every now and then, she would glance coyly at Zack, but he was gazing at Sharon, with interest.

He pulled his chair closer to hers, and spoke in a low, confidential tone. "You know, I'm a little worried about the advisor for this project."

"Mr. Russell? Why?"

"He's new. He won't know the score."

"What score?" Sharon asked.

"The way things happen around here. Look, what I'm saying is that we could do some behind-the-scenes planning and decide what this is going to be all about."

"I think I'd rather wait and see what Mr. Russell's ideas are," Sharon said.

"You want to get together this weekend and talk?" he persisted, as if he hadn't heard her.

"Why can't we just talk here?" Sharon asked. Then it hit her that she was being incredibly naive. The half-closed eyes, the low voice, the suggestive smile—he was coming on to her!

She supposed she should be flattered. Zack was awfully good-looking, if you liked the preppie type. He was a bit too groomed for her taste. She knew he'd been a class president for two years, but that didn't impress her much.

She was attempting to formulate a kind rejection when Debra gave her a sharp kick on her leg.

"I didn't say anything!" she yelped. Then she realized why Debra had demanded her attention. Tyler was coming into the room.

Sharon waved. She moved her chair closer to Debra, creating a space between herself and Zack, and making it clear that she was inviting Tyler to fill it. He did.

"What are you doing here?" Sharon asked.

Tyler spoke too casually. "I thought this sounded more interesting than the *News.*"

"Yeah, me, too," Sharon said. "That's a coincidence."

Tyler seemed totally incapable of meeting her eyes. "Right."

It was on the tip of her tongue to point out that he must have seen her name on the sign-up sheet, but she controlled herself. "Oh, by the way, my family's not going to Savannah this weekend after all."

Finally, he faced her. "Does that mean we're on for Saturday night?"

She nodded, and she was rewarded with a look of real happiness in Tyler's face. The door to the room opened, and she turned to see an unfamiliar girl dressed in black coming in. She was staring at her feet as she ambled over to a chair.

44

"Excuse me," Kris chirped. "This is a meeting. For the cable TV show."

"Yeah, I know." The girl pulled the chair away from the group and sat down. She raised her head briefly to reveal what seemed to be a permanent scowl, and then resumed examining her boot-clad feet.

"Who's that?" Tyler asked Sharon in a whisper.

"I don't know," Sharon replied. She studied the girl with frank curiosity. The punk look wasn't totally unfamiliar to her; there were lots of kids like that in Atlanta. But it certainly wasn't a common sight at Greenwood. In a way, she admired the girl. It took guts to show up at school looking so different from everyone.

Kris began to fidget. "When is this meeting supposed to start?"

"Five minutes ago," Zack said. "And I don't think we should waste our time waiting for advisors who don't care enough to show up." He rose, but just at that moment, Mr. Russell burst in, and Zack sat back down.

"Sorry I'm late, folks," Mr. Russell said. "I was on the phone with Channel 42. We're arranging for them to send over a real crew, to set up the lights and mikes. They're going to take care of all the technical details until some students are trained to take their places." He was rubbing his hands together gleefully as he surveyed the barren room. "We're going to turn this place into a real studio. Knock out that wall, set up bleachers for the audience . . ."

"Audience?" Debra asked. "Is this going to be like one of those TV talk shows?"

"If you want," the teacher said. "It's your show. You're going to decide the format."

Zack's expression was skeptical. "What's your job?"

"I'll provide advice and guidance when you want it. I worked in television before I went into teaching. I can act as director until one of you feels ready to take over."

Zack leaned back in his chair with a satisfied smile, as if he was ready to take over immediately.

"Now, do we all know each other?" Mr. Russell asked. "Let's take a moment for introductions. For those of you who aren't in any of my English classes, I'm Jeff Russell."

Each student in turn gave his or her name. The last to speak was the girl in black, and she mumbled something.

"I'm sorry, I didn't hear you," Mr. Russell said.

She jerked up her head. "Jade Barrow," she snapped. "I'm new, I'm a transfer, I'm a junior. Anything else you have to know about me?"

Sharon had no idea why the girl sounded so hostile, but Mr. Russell didn't seem disturbed by her tone. "I have a feeling we're all going to get to know each other pretty well," he said. "So I think we should *all* be on a first name basis."

Sharon beamed. This was the first time in her memory that a teacher had invited students to use his first name.

"Now, let me tell you what we've got here.

46

We're going to produce a one-hour television show which will appear on Channel 42, weekly."

"You mean, the show isn't just for Greenwood students?" Kris asked.

"Nope. Anyone in the Atlanta metropolitan area with a basic cable connection can tune in. The idea is that it's a show made by teens for teens. The first show will be a test. If it's successful, and if Channel 42 agrees, we'll be doing a show every week. Now, they want the first show to air in three weeks, so we need to make some major decisions today."

"Is it a live show?" Tyler asked.

"No, it'll be taped."

Jade muttered something.

"What did you say?" Jeff asked.

"I said, it figures."

"What do you mean?"

"Well, if it's taped, that means someone can edit it, right? In case anyone says something . . . *naughty.*" She punctuated the word with a nasty smirk.

Jeff considered her remark. "The editor at the station *would* probably bleep out obscenities. But as far as the subjects go, there aren't any no-nos."

He opened his briefcase and pulled out some papers. "According to the grant, and I quote, 'the program will deal with the issues and concerns of today's youth, in a format that can include debates, interviews, presentations, and group discussions.' That's it. No restrictions. No taboos. So, what topics do you think we should deal with on the first show?"

Sharon spoke cautiously. "We can talk about . . . anything? Ow!" She rubbed her shin where Debra had kicked her again. What was she supposed to do, remain silent the whole meeting?

But once again, the kick had been only a warning. Mr. Quimby was walking in. He nodded briefly toward Jeff and then turned to the students.

"Since this is a new activity here at Greenwood, and I'm in charge of all school activities, I thought I'd take a moment from my schedule to welcome you. Student participation in extracurricular activities can be a rewarding and fulfilling experience. It will extend your education beyond the classroom, and offer the opportunity to broaden your horizons."

He spoke in a bored monotone. Obviously, he made the same remarks at every meeting of a new organization.

But then his tone shifted, from bland to grim. "Of course, this particular activity has far-reaching implications. What you will do on this show of yours will be seen by people outside of school. That means you've got a serious responsibility."

He paused for dramatic emphasis. "You will be representing Greenwood High School. People watching you will think, 'these are typical Greenwood students.' What you say, how you behave, even what you wear will be significant."

His eyes darted around, and Sharon saw real pain on his face when those eyes settled on Jade. "So think about what you're going to do and say, how you're going to act, and how others will perceive you. I don't want this show to create any problems."

Somehow, he managed to produce something that vaguely resembled a smile, and barked "good luck," before he started toward the door. He paused when he got there, and looked back.

"These are all the students you've got?" he asked Jeff.

"So far," Jeff replied.

Quimby nodded and made a 'humph' sound. "Well, you'll probably lose your funding."

There was a moment of silence after he walked out. Then Debra spoke quietly. "Do you still think we won't have any taboos, Mr. Russell, I mean, Jeff?"

"No taboos," Jeff said firmly.

A shiver of anticipation shot through Sharon. If Jeff Russell wasn't going to let Quimby call the shots, this show could really be something special. She felt as if she would explode if she didn't get a chance to present her idea soon. But Jeff was still speaking.

"Mr. Quimby made a good point, though. If we don't get more students involved, we could lose the grant. As I told you before, we have three weeks to prepare the first show. But six students aren't enough to prepare weekly shows. What I'm hoping is that once students see the first show, they'll be so impressed they'll all want to be a part of it. So the first show has to be fantastic. Now let's hear some ideas."

Sharon started to put her hand up but Kris beat her to it. "I think we should do interviews."

"With who?" Jeff asked.

"The homecoming queen candidates."

Jade made a loud gagging sound. Sharon avoided Debra's eyes and prayed that this idiotic suggestion wouldn't send her friend flying out the door. She was surprised to see that Jeff seemed to be taking Kris's idea seriously, and this encouraged Kris to continue.

"The students elect the queen, and kids are always saying they can't decide who to vote for because they don't know the girls. It turns into nothing more than a beauty contest."

Tyler stared at her. "What else is it *supposed* to be?"

"A popularity contest!"

"Do you think there's an audience for this beyond Greenwood students?" Jeff asked. "There are at least thirty high schools in the Atlanta area, remember."

Sharon was stunned when she heard Debra say, "I don't think it's a bad idea. I saw one of those magazine shows on TV recently, and they had a segment on the selection of a prom queen at some high school somewhere. It was kind of interesting, actually. And it came right after a segment on conflicts in the Middle East, so it kept the whole show from being too heavy."

Jeff went to the free-standing blackboard, fished a stick of chalk from his pocket, and wrote 'homecoming queen interviews.' "Okay, more ideas."

"For a serious topic," Zack said, "I'd like to propose preparing for the SATs."

"That's not serious," Tyler said. "It's depressing. And if we want to get a lot of attention with this first show, we need to do something that's a little more, you know, *hot.*"

Sharon looked at him with approval. He was really getting into this! "In fact," Tyler continued, "I think Sharon's got a great idea."

I could love this guy, Sharon thought, as Jeff said, "Let's hear it, Sharon."

At last! Sharon took a deep breath. "I think a hot topic would be this condom controversy."

She paused. Zack was looking at her as if she was a space alien. There was horror on Kris's face. She *thought* she saw a flicker of interest in Jade's eyes. But she focused her attention on Jeff and launched into her prepared speech.

"We all know about the dangers of AIDS, and according to statistics, it's spreading among people our age. They keep telling us that condoms provide the best protection. But when it was proposed over in Fulton County that high schools should start distributing condoms for free in the school clinics, some people threw a fit. It's going to come up at the next school board meeting here in Dekalb County, and I think this show would be a great place for kids to give *their* opinion."

The room was deadly silent. She searched Jeff's face for a reaction. "What do the rest of you think?" he asked.

"I think it's *disgusting!*" Kris blurted out. "You heard what Mr. Quimby said. We'll be representing Greenwood. If we start saying we think kids here need . . . those *things*, that's the same as saying we're all, you know . . ."

"Having sex?" Jade finished. "You mean, you're not?" She slumped deeper into her chair. "Oh, great. I'm trapped in a school for virgins."

"I agree with Kris," Zack said quickly. "Like Mr. Quimby said, this could create problems."

"I like the idea," Debra argued. "It's controversial, and it'll attract audiences."

"And it's important," Tyler added.

"Important to who?" Zack retorted. "As far as I know we haven't had any cases of AIDS here at Greenwood."

"Yeah, well, maybe there've been cases at *other* high schools," Tyler shot back.

"There have." That came from Jade. "Of course, having sex isn't the only way you can get AIDS. You can get it from sharing needles. Junkies get AIDS."

Was she just trying to shock them, Sharon wondered. She didn't care if she was. Jade seemed to be on her side.

"Condoms help prevent pregnancy, too," Debra said. "And I'm sure we've had cases of *that* here."

Up until now, Jeff's face had been impassive. He'd listened, and nodded, but he hadn't given any indication of how he felt about the subject.

Now, finally, he smiled. "I like this. I like it a lot."

Kris was aghast. "You *do?*"

"Just listening to all of you tells me this is a perfect subject," Jeff said. "It affects your lives.

52

You're excited, you've got opinions, and that means the audience will have strong reactions, too."

He went to the blackboard, and wrote 'condoms.' Then he turned back to them, and grinned broadly. "Folks, I think we've got a show."

Four

"What are you calling your show?" Sharon's mother asked, sinking into an armchair with a cup of tea.

"We haven't come up with a title yet," Debra told her. She was curled up at one end of the sofa, and Sharon sat at the other end. A soft rain tapped at the windows of the living-room. It was Saturday afternoon, and the girls had just returned from the public library.

"We've been doing research all morning," Sharon said.

"What kind of research?" Mrs. Delaney asked.

Debra suddenly became very interested in her fingernails. But Sharon knew her mother could handle this.

"AIDS in adolescence, and condoms," she said.

Her mother nodded in approval. "And you're going to talk about this on your show? Very topical."

"Sharon's appearing on the show," Debra said. "I'm just doing behind the scenes work. Which is exactly what I want to do."

"It's not just me on the show," Sharon told her mother. "We're discussing whether or not condoms should be distributed at school. I'm taking one side of the issue and Zack Stevenson's taking the other side."

"Which side are you on?"

"Oh, Mom, can't you guess? I'm pro, Zack's con."

"Zack Stevenson . . ." her mother repeated. "Is that Senator Stevenson's son?"

Debra nodded. "And he doesn't let anyone forget it. Sharon, remember when he was running for student body president? His whole campaign was based on the idea that just because his father's in politics, he knows everything."

"It certainly didn't help him," Sharon said. To her mother, she added, "He lost."

"Well, if his politics are anything like his father's, you're all better off," Mrs. Delaney commented. "That man doesn't want to spend a dime on any program related to education, or welfare, on anything *meaningful*. In fact, he's one of the officials who's opposed to the condom plan."

Sharon wasn't surprised. "Personally, I don't see how anyone can be against giving out condoms. If they can protect us from AIDS . . ."

"Pregnancy, too," Debra commented. "Not that *I* need to worry about that," she added quickly.

"Well, I think it's marvelous that the school's allowing you to discuss this," Mrs. Delaney stated. "After all, you kids are the ones who are affected by these decisions. Your opinions should be heard. Is the whole show going to be about the condom controversy?"

"I wish," Sharon sighed. "But there's another segment." She made a face.

"Don't pout," Debra remonstrated. "Remember, we've got to attract as many viewers as possible. Some kids are more interested in homecoming queens than condoms."

"Homecoming queens?"

"Kris Hogan is interviewing the candidates," Sharon said. She turned to Debra. "Weren't you surprised when Jade volunteered to do the research on that?"

"How much research do you think there is to do?" Debra replied. "She just wants to get by with doing as little work as possible."

"I still can't figure out why she's even involved with this show," Sharon remarked.

Debra grinned wickedly. "Maybe it's a condition of probation."

"Who's Jade?" Mrs. Delaney asked.

"Jade Barrow," Sharon said. "She's new, a transfer. But she acts like she's just been released from reform school. Punk, with a real attitude." After a pause, she said, "I wonder what she's really like. I have a feeling she's putting on an act."

Mrs. Delaney drained the last of her tea, and rose. "Well, it sounds like you've got an interesting show. Condoms and homecoming queens. Are there many other students working on the show?"

"Just Tyler," Sharon said.

"Your Tyler?"

"Mom! He's not *my* Tyler. We've only had one date."

"But you've got a second one, tonight," Debra noted. "What are you wearing?"

"I haven't even thought about it."

Debra shook her head in amusement. "Oh, stop trying to act like you don't care. Come on, let's go raid your closet. Want to join us, Mrs. Delaney?"

"I wish I could, but I've got a stack of essays to grade." She scooped up a thick folder with Emory University emblazoned across the front. "But if you move on to *my* closet, give me some warning."

The girls ran upstairs to Sharon's room. There, Debra went directly to the closet, while Sharon threw herself on the bed. "I am *so* excited!"

"About your date tonight?"

"About the show, dummy!" She sat up. "We have *got* to come up with a cool title. You have any brilliant ideas?"

"Not at the moment." She turned and faced Sharon, hands on her hips. "Aren't you the least bit excited about Tyler? You do like him, don't you?"

Sharon gave an elaborate shrug and kept her voice light. "Oh, sure, I like him." She was trying to sound terribly casual, but she could feel the small smile playing about her lips. "Of course, I don't really know him all that well yet. And I don't believe in love at first sight."

Debra turned back to the closet, but Sharon didn't miss her soft, "*I* do."

Sharon watched her friend rummage through the clothes. Debra never dated, and she'd never seemed concerned about love before. "Maybe Tyler knows someone to fix you up with. A senior."

"No, thanks," Debra replied. "I'm not interested in *dating.* I want to be in *love.*"

"But how are you going to fall in love if you don't date?" Sharon argued.

"I'll know Mr. Right when I see him," Debra said. "I can wait until then. Meanwhile, I'll get my kicks from your relationship, okay?"

"It's fine with me. You know what you are, Debra? A closet romantic."

"Speaking of closets," Debra said pointedly.

Sharon dragged herself off the bed and joined her. "I hate this weather. I'm sick of summer clothes and it's too warm to wear anything else."

"What about this?" Debra asked, pulling at a striped tank dress.

"It makes me look fat."

A pale peach baby-doll dress came out next. "This is nice."

"It looked good when I had a tan," Sharon said. "Deb, do you think Tyler's cute?"

"Very."

"I think he's smart, too. Not intellectual, maybe, but smarter than he acts. And he doesn't put on an obnoxious macho act, like a lot of guys. He doesn't strut around like he's some heavenly gift to the female species. And he's got a sense of humor that's not goofy."

58

"You like him," Debra stated flatly. "A lot."

Sharon bit her lip. "I think . . . maybe . . . I *could*. I want to get to know him. I have a feeling he's got a lot of interesting things going on in his life that he doesn't let everyone know about. There's something in his eyes . . ."

"And you're calling *me* a romantic!" Debra pulled a dress from the closet. The price tag was still attached. "This is it."

Sharon considered the soft, slinky dress, with its rust and gold floral print. "I've been saving that."

"For what? This is your second date. Second dates are when things start getting serious. Or so I've heard."

Sharon hung the dress on the hook outside the closet door, and then got down on her knees to search for shoes to go with it. "Deb, when you say serious, do you mean what I think you mean?"

"Like, is Tyler going to jump your bones tonight?"

"Debra!" Sharon found her simple brown flats and pulled herself upright. "You know, even though I'm totally in favor of handing out condoms at school, I wonder how many kids really need them. Personally, I think all these reports of sexually active adolescents are exaggerated."

"Some kids are definitely sexually active," Debra noted. "Remember Vickie Gilligan?"

Sharon recalled their classmate from last year. According to rumor, she'd been pregnant and had an abortion.

59

"And Molly what's-her-name, the senior," Debra went on. "She had a baby this summer. I've seen her walking around with the stroller."

"They might be unique, though," Sharon commented. "And that's why we've heard about them."

"No one *I* know is having sex," Debra said. "Of course, I don't know that many people well enough to talk about it. You'll have to ask around, find out what's really going on."

"Oh, right. I'm going to go up to people and say, 'excuse me, are you having sex?' "

Debra giggled. "I guess you'll have to be a little more tactful than that. Or maybe you won't have to ask. Just listen. Didn't you say Tyler was taking you to some party tonight?"

"Yeah."

"Keep your ears open," Debra advised. "You might learn something."

Sharon scrutinized herself in the mirror. Her freshly washed hair gleamed, and the time she'd taken to put on eye makeup paid off. She'd actually managed to achieve a little sophistication.

She stepped back to get more perspective on her reflection. The dress was good—not too casual, not too dressy. She had no idea what the other girls would be wearing tonight. The party was at the home of one of Tyler's friends, and she supposed most of the kids there would be seniors. She didn't want to look too . . . *junior.*

Her own thoughts made her smile. She couldn't

remember the last time she'd fussed so much about a date. Of course, she could barely remember the last time she'd *had* a date.

She fingered the deep scoop neckline of the dress. Did she look too bare? She left her room and went downstairs to the kitchen, where Kyle and her father were on dish duty, and her mother was still grading essays at the breakfast table.

"Mom, do you think I need something here?" She indicated the front of her dress.

"Yeah," Kyle piped up. "Boobs."

Sharon considered shrieking but decided it was best to ignore the brat. Her parents didn't, though.

"Don't make personal comments like that," Mr. Delaney admonished.

"And they're not called 'boobs,' they're breasts," Mrs. Delaney added. "Use the proper words."

Personally, Sharon thought her own were so minuscule they didn't deserve names at all, but she just shot one swift dirty look at her brother and muttered, "sexist pig."

Kyle just grinned, tossed his dish towel onto the rack, and sauntered out.

"It's unbelievable," Sharon complained. "He's only twelve years old and he's already got sex on his mind."

"No, he doesn't," her mother said comfortably. "He's just showing off." She examined Sharon's dress. "I've got a necklace that might look good."

Sharon followed her up to the master bedroom, where her mother began searching through her jewelry box. "Tyler seems like a nice boy," she commented. "Of course, I only met him briefly."

"He is," Sharon murmured, shaking her head at a necklace her mother offered. "That's too chunky."

"Do you like him?"

"Yeah."

Mrs. Delaney handed her a thin, twisted gold chain, and spoke slowly. "Sharon, you know what we were talking about this afternoon . . ."

Sharon held the necklace at her neck. "Yes?"

"I don't mean to pry, but . . . do you carry protection with you?"

Sharon was so shocked she dropped the necklace down the front of her dress. "Do you honestly think I *need* protection?" she asked as she fished the chain out.

"I'm just trying to be a modern mother," Mrs. Delaney protested. "I read the articles. I know that teenagers are having sex."

"Not *all* teenagers. Not *this* one."

She didn't miss the relief that crossed her mother's face. "But when you do decide to, well, become seriously involved with someone . . ."

Sharon patted her mother's shoulder. "Don't worry, Mom. I'm not stupid. Thanks for the necklace."

She went back to her bedroom for her handbag. Parents, she thought, could be so naive. They believed *everything* they read and heard.

She was halfway down the stairs when she heard the doorbell. She hesitated. Should she, wait here, let someone else answer it, and then make an entrance? No, that was ridiculous. Girls like Kris Hogan probably did things like that. She wasn't going to play those kind of games.

She ran down the stairs, tore past her parents, and beat her brother to the door.

"Hi, come on in," she greeted Tyler breathlessly.

"Hi, how're you doing?" he asked.

"Fine."

She watched as he greeted her parents, and for the second time, she admired the way he was able to talk to them without mumbling and shuffling his feet, like some guys would. He said all the right things, and even remembered to ask Kyle about his soccer team.

When they left the house, he held the door open for her. Which wasn't necessary, of course—she was perfectly capable of opening her own door. Still, it was nice to be treated like she was special.

"Who's giving this party?" she asked as they settled into his old Ford.

"Gary Felder. His parents are out of town."

"I don't think I know him," Sharon said.

"He's . . . well, I've known him practically all my life, but he's turned into kind of a jerk. So if he says something really stupid—"

"That's okay," Sharon assured him. "I know lots of jerks, too." She wrinkled her nose. "Zack Stevenson . . ."

"He won't be there," Tyler assured her. "He runs with a different crowd. Country Club types, debutantes, private school kids."

63

"I wonder why he's not in private school," Sharon mused.

"Because of his father. It's uncool for politicians to send their kids to private schools. Poor Zack . . ."

Sharon was surprised by the show of sympathy. "I think he's a jerk."

"He is," Tyler agreed. "But maybe that's not all his fault. Can you imagine what it must be like to have a father like Senator Stevenson? I'll bet Zack's under a lot of pressure. That could be why he's such a show-off."

Sharon was impressed with Tyler's show of sensitivity. But she didn't want to learn more about Zack as much as she wanted to know more about Tyler. She was trying to come up with a discreet way of asking him about himself when he took his eyes off the road just long enough to give her a big smile. "You look great."

"Thanks. So do you."

He seemed pleasantly surprised by that remark. "You know, I think that's the first time a girl's said that to me. I mean, guys are always complimenting girls, telling them how nice they look, but you hardly ever hear girls complimenting guys. Why do you think that is?"

"Sex roles and stereotypes," Sharon replied promptly. "Guys think that girls spend ages getting ready for a date, and guys are supposed to show they appreciate all the effort. A girl doesn't compliment a guy, because she figures all the guy did was take a shower, comb his hair, and throw on some clothes."

"How about you?" Tyler asked. "Did you spend ages getting ready for this date?"

"Not *ages*. But . . . well, yeah, I made an effort to look nice. How about you?"

"I took a shower, combed my hair, and threw on my clothes."

She tossed her head back and laughed, and he joined in. They joked around all the way to Gary Felder's house. When they arrived, it was clear that a party was going on. All the lights in the house were on, there were cars crowding the driveway and lined up on the street, and even as they stood out on the sidewalk, they could hear the music blaring.

Tyler knocked, waited a moment, and then opened the door. Inside, it was obvious no one would have heard the knocking. The noise was deafening. From the foyer, Sharon could see into the living-room, where kids covered the furniture and couples were dancing. On the other side of the foyer was the dining room, where others were devouring pizza.

A good-looking boy with longish black hair appeared. "Hey, buddy."

"Hiya, pal. This is Sharon. Sharon, Gary."

"Nice to meet you," Sharon said.

"Same here, babe."

Sharon flinched. She hated that word. She felt Tyler's hand tighten on hers, and she managed a thin smile.

Gary took off. "I told you he was a jerk," Tyler said, and Sharon knew Tyler would never call her 'babe.' They wandered into the living-room.

Sharon was relieved to see a couple of girls she knew from the junior class, and they waved to each other. Then the party fell into a typical Greenwood High party pattern. She and Tyler danced, then separated to gather with same-sex friends. They returned to dance, and then separated again.

She commented on this routine the next time she huddled with the girls. "Why does this always happen?"

Lori shrugged. "Guys want to talk to guys, girls want to talk to girls."

"But why can't we talk to each other?" Sharon persisted. "Why can't we be friends?"

"Girls and guys *can't* be friends," Sandra stated.

Beth Ann snorted. "Yeah, guys don't want to talk to us, they only want to do it to us."

Sharon remembered her earlier conversation with Debra. Here was an opening. "Do you think guys are more interested in having sex than girls?"

"Depends on the girl," Beth Ann said with a wink. She opened her purse, and revealed a round plastic case. "Birth control pills," she told them. "Of course, I make Andy use condoms. Double protection."

Sharon couldn't say she was all that surprised. Beth Ann had been going with the same senior for over a year. But she glanced at the others, and tried to read their reactions.

No one looked shocked, or dismayed. She wondered if they were on the pill, too. She couldn't get up the nerve to come right out and ask them.

Beth Ann didn't have that problem. "What about you and Tyler?"

"What about us?"

"Are you doing it?"

Sharon tried to sound nonchalant. "Beth Ann, it's only our second date."

"He's awfully cute," Sandra commented. "*I* wouldn't mind."

"Take a number," Lori said. "I wouldn't mind, either."

Sharon knew she was being teased. She could handle it. "You guys *better* mind, as long as I'm around," she said, raising a fist in a mock fighting position.

The girls split up to find their dates. Sharon looked around, but she didn't see Tyler. She wondered if her eye makeup was holding up, and decided to check it out.

The bathroom off the foyer was occupied, so she went upstairs. There were several doors off the hallway, and all were closed. She took a chance and opened one.

It wasn't a bathroom. It was a bedroom, and it was occupied, too. In the dark, Sharon made out two forms, moving together on the bed. Quickly and silently, she closed the door.

The next one turned out to be a bathroom. She went in, turned on the light, and closed the door.

Rubbing the smudge of mascara from under her eye, she thought about what she'd just witnessed. Seniors, probably, she decided. But maybe not. Beth Ann was a junior, and she was having sex. Of course, Beth Ann could have been just showing off, like her kid brother. And none of the other girls had whipped birth control pills out of their handbags.

She left the bathroom and ran right into Tyler.

"There you are!" he exclaimed. "I've been looking for you."

"Here I am," she said brightly.

"Nice house, huh? I want to show you something."

Sharon held her breath as he moved toward the door she'd accidentally opened. But he passed it, and opened the next one.

"I've *seen* bedrooms, Tyler," she said dryly.

"No, come here, look." He opened the door wider.

It was a little den, with the biggest TV screen Sharon had ever seen. It covered half the wall.

"Wow, it's like a private movie theater," Sharon commented. "And look at that stereo!"

"Yeah, it's the best you can buy," Tyler told her. "It's a shame Gary wastes this great equipment on his CDs. I think he's got every heavy metal album made."

"What kind of music do you like?" Sharon asked.

He named some bands, and she was pleased to learn that they shared the same taste in music. She was awed at the intelligent way he could talk about the bands.

"You know a lot about music," she commented.

He reddened a little. "Well, I fool around a little myself. With a guitar." He gave her a look that seemed almost anxious, like he wasn't sure whether to go on.

She encouraged him. "What do you like to play?"

"My own stuff, mostly. I've written some songs."

"I'd love to hear them," Sharon said. "Unless you want to keep them private. My friend Debra writes poetry, but she doesn't like to talk about it or show it to anyone. I guess it's the same with music, for some people."

"I don't talk about it much," Tyler admitted. He paused. "But, maybe, sometime . . . I could play some for you."

Sharon felt a warm glow. She could tell he considered his music something very personal and very important. But he wanted to share it with her! "I'd like that," she said.

Now Tyler looked a little flustered, like he was afraid he'd exposed too much. He opened a cabinet. There must have been a hundred video cassettes in there. "When Gary and I were in Little League, the whole team would come over here after practice and watch movies. You ever seen a video on a screen this big? It's not like watching on regular TV."

Sharon was examining the cassettes. "Ooh, *Casablanca*. I think that's the most romantic movie in the world."

"Guess we'd better go back to the party," Tyler said.

"Okay."

"Or we could stay in here and watch *Casablanca*." He smiled sheepishly. "I'm not really much of a party animal."

Which gave Sharon a reason to like him even more. "Neither am I."

Tyler turned on the TV, and inserted the cassette. They settled back on the couch, side by side.

Even though Sharon had seen the film before, she found herself totally absorbed in it again. It was so romantic, beautiful and sad, full of longing and desire and heartache. When Tyler draped his arm around her, she automatically rested her head on his chest. The mood was perfect. And when he turned her face toward his, and they kissed, it was comfortable. It felt right.

They continued to kiss, and his hand moved around her back. She was dimly aware of sensations that grew in intensity as time passed. At first, it was nice. Then he placed a hand on her knee, and slowly moved it upward, under her dress.

She placed her own hand on top of his, and gently pushed it away. He buried his face in her hair, and whispered, "Come on." The hand started moving again.

"Don't," she said softly.

"It's okay."

This time she removed the hand a little less gently. "It's *not* okay."

He got the message, and pulled back. There was a hint of a scowl on his face. Sharon didn't know what to say. Was he angry, she wondered. She considered apologizing, but for what? For not doing something that didn't feel right?

She glanced back at the TV screen. The main characters were locked in a passionate kiss. Maybe this wasn't such a perfect movie to be watching right now, she thought.

Tyler seemed to be getting the same idea. "Are you hungry?" he asked.

"A little," she admitted.

"I'm starving," he said. "Let's go see if there's any pizza left."

She waited by the door while he stopped the video, ejected the cassette, and replaced it. When he turned back toward her, he smiled.

Reassured, she smiled back. Everything was okay, she decided. For now.

Five

"And then what happened?" Debra asked.

Sitting across the table from Debra in the media center early Monday morning, Sharon drummed her fingers on the fat reference book. "We've only got forty-five minutes before the bell, and we need to go through this index."

But for once, Debra was more concerned with something other than books. She was still fixated on Sharon's report of her date. "Was Tyler angry?"

"About what?"

"When you wouldn't let him go any further."

"I don't think so. He asked me to go to the football game with him Friday."

"I wonder if he actually expected you to go all the way," Debra mused.

"Keep your voice down," Sharon hissed, glancing around the room. "I don't think the whole world needs to know about my sex life."

"But you're going to be asking everyone else about theirs," Debra pointed out.

Sometimes, Debra could be just too matter-of-fact. The direction of the conversation was making Sharon uncomfortable. "Look, there's Kris," she said, glad for a distraction.

Kris was off her crutches now, but she was still limping a little. She spotted them, and came over to their table. "Have you seen Carl Perez?"

"Who's Carl Perez?" Debra asked.

Sharon thought Debra was probably the only student at Greenwood who wouldn't recognize that name. "He's captain of the football team," she informed her. To Kris, she said, "No, I haven't seen him. Why?"

"He's supposed to meet me here," Kris told them. "I want to find out exactly how the candidates for homecoming queen are selected."

"Isn't that Jade's job, to do the background work?" Debra asked.

Kris shook her head in annoyance. "I can't count on her to do anything. I don't think she's done one bit of research."

"I'm going to the school board meeting tonight," Sharon announced. "They're going to discuss the condom issue."

"That's nice," Kris said vaguely. "Ooh, there's Carl now." She waved to the big, handsome guy who was walking into the media center.

As Kris limped away, Debra muttered, "Research on homecoming queens."

"Speaking of research," Sharon said, "let's get to work."

* * *

73

As they sat down at a table, Kris hit Carl with her best smile, even though she knew there wasn't much point in flirting with him. He was known to be totally committed to his girlfriend, Tracy, one of the homecoming queen candidates. Still, it couldn't hurt.

Carl fidgeted in his seat. "How's your ankle?"

"Better," Kris told him. "But I'll be off the cheerleading squad for the whole season."

"That's too bad," Carl said. "What did you want to talk to me about?"

"I'm working on this new cable TV show," Kris told him, "and I'm going to interview the homecoming queen candidates."

"Cool," Carl said, and shifted his position again.

"I thought you could give me some background. I know that the football team chooses the candidates. How do they decide who to pick?"

"It's pretty loose," Carl said. "Anyone on the team can nominate a girl. Then we vote on all of them, and the four who get the most votes are the candidates."

"I see." Kris made a note of this process. "I'll bet some of the guys must put a lot of pressure on the others to vote for their girlfriends."

"Nah, it's secret ballot."

"Still," Kris pressed, "it must help if a girl is going with a team member."

"Not really. *You* were nominated."

Kris almost dropped her pen. "You're kidding!"

"Nope."

74

She giggled in an effort to mask her amazement. "How many votes did I get?"

"I don't remember exactly," Carl said. "But I know you came in fifth. Look, do you have any other questions? 'Cause I gotta go."

"No, I think that's all I need," Kris said. "Thank you very much, Carl."

Carl left the table, but Kris remained, staring into space. Her head was spinning and her mind was racing.

She knew she was pretty, and she knew she was generally popular. She'd gone out with guys on the team. But she'd never dared to consider herself as a possible candidate for homecoming queen. Of the four girls nominated, only one was a junior, and that was Tracy, the captain's girlfriend. The three others were the prettiest, most popular seniors at Greenwood.

To know that she'd received the fifth highest number of votes—what an honor! Next to prom queen or Miss Greenwood High, homecoming queen was just about the most prestigious title a girl could attain. Just to have come this close to a nomination told her how far she'd come from being poor, low-rent trash.

For a few moments, she just sat there, reveling in the knowledge that she was even more popular, more accepted, than she'd thought she was.

Then, slowly, the thrill began to evaporate. She had come so close to being a candidate, maybe only one or two votes behind number four. If just *one* of those four girls hadn't been nominated, she'd be a candidate for homecoming queen.

Not that she could have become the actual queen. Homecoming queens were always seniors. But she could have been standing on that platform at half-time in the homecoming game, sharing the attention with only three others. Her picture would have been on a special page of the annual yearbook. It would have made up for not being a cheerleader. It was even better than cheerleading—as cheerleader, she shared the spotlight with *nine* other girls.

She'd come so close . . . but coming in fifth meant nothing. No one, except for the football team, would even know. Suddenly, she was depressed. And there was nothing she could do about it. Of course, there was always the remote possibility that one of the four might drop out of the running, and she'd take her place. Or maybe someone's grades might slip; she might be put on probation and declared ineligible. But that wasn't very likely.

The blues hung over her like a heavy rain cloud. She had to get rid of them before anyone noticed. She was bouncy, bubbly Kris Hogan, with a reputation to maintain. She tried to channel her depression elsewhere, turn it into something else.

The TV show . . . . She thought about Jade, who wasn't doing her work. She decided to find her and scold her for this. She left the media center and went to the hallway where most of the juniors had their lockers.

It was easy picking out Jade among all the students lining the hall. Didn't she ever change her clothes, Kris wondered. Automatically, her nose wrinkled. She didn't want passing kids to see her talking to this wacko.

She edged closer to the locker where Jade was twisting the combination, and spoke out of the corner of her mouth. "I need to talk to you."

"Talk," Jade said, jerking the locker open.

"Not here." Kris thought rapidly. "Meet me in the restroom around the corner." She waited only long enough to see Jade nod. Then she walked as fast as her bad ankle would allow. She'd picked that particular restroom since it had no mirrors, and girls never used it unless they were desperate.

As she'd hoped, the restroom was deserted. A few seconds after Kris's arrival, Jade sauntered in. She perched herself on the edge of a sink, and pulled a crumpled pack of cigarettes from the back pocket of her ripped jeans.

"What do you want?" Jade extracted a cigarette and stuck it in her mouth.

Kris glanced nervously toward the door, expecting a teacher to burst in at any moment. "Would you mind not doing that? I hate to breathe cigarette smoke."

"Then don't breathe." Jade struck a match, lit the cigarette, and exhaled a heavy stream of smoke.

Nasty, disgusting girl, Kris thought. She coughed delicately. But she didn't make a fuss. Because in the back of her mind, an idea was forming. And if she was going to turn this idea into a plan, she would need Jade's help.

"Have you done any work for the program?" she asked.

"Nope."

"You're *supposed* to be doing research," Kris said sternly.

"Research on homecoming queens?" Jade uttered a short, harsh laugh.

"Well, you could get some facts about their lives. Where they were born, if they have brothers and sisters . . ."

Jade took the cigarette out of her mouth long enough to say, "Boring."

That gave Kris an opening. "Yes, you're probably right. No one really cares about stuff like that. But we *do* need some kind of information about the girls."

"You're doing the interview on TV," Jade said. "You can get all the information you want then."

"But I need to know something about them *first* so I can make up the right kind of questions," Kris argued.

"Like what? Their *hobbies?*"

"No." Kris formulated her next statement with care. "I want to know the stuff they won't want to tell me on TV."

Jade's clear blue eyes narrowed. "Why?"

Kris spoke lightly. "Oh, it could be more entertaining that way. You know, like those gossip shows on TV. If I could know something . . . *personal* about the girls, I could ask them more interesting questions."

"You want the dirt," Jade said bluntly.

Kris didn't say yes. But she didn't say no, either.

"How am I supposed to get this information?" Jade asked. "They're not going to tell *me* their secrets."

"Talk to people who know them," Kris suggested. "I'll make a list for you, of their friends."

Jade hopped off the sink, and tossed the cigarette into a toilet. "I've got a better idea. Make me a list of their enemies."

Kris nodded and smiled. "No problem."

"There's a space," Sharon announced, as she drove the car slowly through the Greenwood parking lot.

"It looks awfully small," Mrs. Delaney warned her.

"I can make it," Sharon said confidently. She maneuvered the car carefully into the tight space. "How's that?"

"Excellent," her mother declared. "You're turning into a fine driver."

They both got out of the car. "I didn't think there would be such a crowd," Sharon remarked, surveying the lot and the people moving toward the gym entrance. "Are all school board meetings this popular?"

"I've only been to one before," her mother murmured. She was gazing toward the school with a frown.

"What's the matter?" Sharon asked. Then she saw what her mother was seeing. "What are the police doing here?" She counted four uniformed officers standing by the entrance to the gym.

"They must be expecting problems," Mrs. Delaney said uneasily. "Sharon, maybe we should pass up this meeting. You'll hear all about it on the news tonight. Or, you can read about it in tomorrow's newspaper."

"Mom, I *have* to go," Sharon insisted. "I don't want to get the information second hand. I need to *see* how people react." She touched her mother's arm. "I'm sure the police are here just as a precaution. Nothing's going to happen."

Mrs. Delaney didn't seem particularly reassured, but she nodded, and they walked to the entrance.

"There's Mrs. Crenshaw," Sharon said, pointing out their next door neighbor.

"Hello, Alice," Mrs. Delaney called.

Their neighbor turned with a smile. "Hi, Jean." Then she stopped smiling. "Sharon! What are you doing here?"

"It's for school," Sharon began, but Mrs. Crenshaw didn't let her finish. "Jean, do you really think Sharon should be here? Do you know what's being discussed tonight?"

Sharon was relieved to see her mother had recovered from her concerns. "Absolutely, Alice. I wish more students were here. After all, this kind of decision affects them."

"Come on, Mom," Sharon urged.

The Greenwood High gym doubled as an auditorium. When it was to be used as an auditorium, the bleachers were pushed flat against the walls, and folding chairs covered the floor. The chairs were almost all filled by the time Sharon and her mother came in, and they couldn't find two together. Sharon sat at the end of one row, while Mrs. Delaney moved down to the middle of the row behind her.

Almost immediately, Sharon wished they had reversed their positions. The vacant chair in front of her held a coat, and its owner soon appeared.

"What are *you* doing here?" Zack asked.

"Same thing you're doing here," Sharon replied. "Getting background for the TV show."

"Actually, I'm here for my father," Zack told her. "He couldn't come, and he likes to know what his constituents are talking about. So he asked me to, you know, represent him."

He was acting as if she should be impressed by this, and she knew she should fake a little awe, to be polite. But she didn't want to encourage his attentions. "That's nice," she murmured, gazing off elsewhere.

Zack became solemn. "Do you really want to be here? The discussion might become a little . . . embarrassing, for a girl."

Sharon raised her eyebrows. "Why would talking about condoms be any more embarrassing for a girl than a boy? Women have to take just as much responsibility for sexual behavior as men. Besides, it was my idea to present this issue on our show, remember?"

Zack's face fell. "Oh. You're one of those feminist types, huh?"

"Absolutely," Sharon replied.

It was a good thing she wasn't the least bit interested romantically in Zack Stevenson. She

81

could see from his expression that whatever appeal she'd had for him was gone. He turned around and faced forward.

Sharon shifted her gaze toward the school board members sitting at the long table on the stage. The man in the center, the school board president, was rapping a gavel. He spoke into a microphone.

"I would like to call this meeting to order." He pressed a handkerchief to his shiny forehead, and Sharon wondered if he could be nervous. "I will ask the secretary to read the minutes from the last meeting."

Another man rose and began to read slowly in a monotone. Sharon took the opportunity to examine the faces in the audience. She recognized a few—some teachers, parents of friends, people from her neighborhood. The unfamiliar ones just seemed like regular people too, nice people, not the kind who would get into fights or start a riot. Personally, she thought the police men outside were totally unnecessary.

The secretary droned on, and the audience wasn't exactly giving him rapt attention. Sharon could see some people having whispered conversations, or leaning back in their chairs with their eyes closed.

The secretary finished, the minutes were approved, and the president spoke again. "Under old business, the first matter concerns cafeteria renovations in two elementary schools. We will now hear a report from the treasurer . . ."

No one in the audience appeared to be terribly

interested in cafeteria renovations. All around the room, people were beginning to murmur and make sounds of exasperation. As the treasurer read her report, the crowd became more and more restless. The murmuring grew louder.

After the board voted to approve the treasurer's recommendations, the president announced, "The next order of old business deals with the custodians' contracts."

Immediately, the murmurs became grumbles, noisy ones, impossible to ignore. The school board tried to continue their discussion, but suddenly, a man rose from the audience. "Get onto the new business!" he bellowed.

Sounds of agreement could be heard throughout the auditorium. The school board members put their hands over their microphones and held a hasty conversation. Then the president spoke again.

"It's been moved that the board table the old business and go on to the first order of new business."

Even from way in the back, Sharon could see that he was really sweating now. And as he spoke, she thought she heard a quiver in his voice.

"It has been recommended that metropolitan high schools take measures in order to prevent the spread of . . ." he coughed, and mopped his brow again. "To prevent the spread of sexually transmitted diseases among adolescents. One of the recommendations states that . . ." he coughed again. "States that condoms be made available to students through the high school health clinics at no cost. We will entertain comments from the audience on this recommendation."

It was then Sharon noticed that there was a standing microphone set up in the aisle that divided the seats. Already, a line was forming behind it.

The first person to speak was a woman. "As a parent, I think this idea is outrageous and completely unnecessary. As far as I'm aware, there have been no reported cases of AIDS at my son's school."

A school board member replied. "And we want to keep it that way. Distributing condoms might help to insure that."

The next speaker, a man, stated, "This is a family matter, not a school matter. What do condoms have to do with education?" He didn't wait for a response, and relinquished the microphone to the next in line.

"I want my tax money spent on books, not condoms!" a man declared.

Sharon recognized the woman who came after him. She was one of the school librarians, and she responded to that comment. "Normally, I'd love to have more money spent on books. But if we don't spend our money to stop this disease, we won't need any books."

A particularly distressed woman took her place. "We should be teaching our kids to abstain from sex!"

Sharon was busily taking notes, so she didn't even notice at first when people stopped going to the microphone and began calling out from their seats.

"Making condoms easy to get will only encourage kids to have sex!"

"They don't need any encouragement. They're already *having* sex!"

"We don't have to condone it!"

"You want your kids to die?"

"This all started with sex education. We should never have allowed sex education in the schools!"

Sex education . . . Sharon had some dim memories of that. In elementary school, they had been taught the parts of the body and how men were different from women. She recalled exchanging winks and grins and muffled giggles with her friends as certain words were said aloud. In middle school, sex education had become more scientific, more technical. They saw films, they heard lectures, they studied diagrams. Everyone was made to understand how it all worked, how it happened.

But nobody ever talked about whether you should or shouldn't do it, or when, or what it meant, or how you might feel.

Caught up in her reflections, Sharon was taken by surprise to realize that people were now yelling, shouting. Voices overlapped, and no one was listening to anyone else. They were venting their own personal furies.

"Don't you have any morals?"

"I'm trying to raise my kids right, and you people are putting ideas into their heads!"

"Safe sex is better than risking death!"

"Schools have no business giving out condoms!"

One of the school board members spoke into her microphone. "I move we close the discussion."

"Forget it!" someone yelled.

Half the audience were out of their seats. Sharon didn't bother to take more notes. She didn't need them. She'd never forget the sounds of anger, the tension, that enveloped the auditorium.

The president of the school board was banging his gavel, calling in vain for order. "The motion to close this discussion has been approved. The vote will not be taken tonight. The meeting is adjourned."

But he might as well have saved his breath. People were still yelling arguing, declaring their opinions passionately.

Sharon felt a hand on her shoulder. Turning, she looked into her mother's pale, anxious face. "Honey, I can't stand this any longer. Let's get out of here."

Behind her mother, Sharon saw that the police had entered the auditorium. They looked tense, too.

"Yeah, okay," Sharon said. Others had started moving toward the exit, and there was a crush at the door. Her mother was being edged out of her row and into the aisle.

"I'll meet you at the car," Sharon called to her. As she rose, so did Zack. He turned around.

"What do you think now?" he asked. "You understand what it's all about?"

"Not really," Sharon replied. "I don't think *anyone* understands what it's all about."

"My father says Greenwood kids don't need free condoms."

"They don't?"

"Nah." He grinned. "Because they can afford to buy their own."

"That's not the point," Sharon said coldly.

"Anyway, my father thinks it's all nonsense," Zack told her.

Sharon studied him. "What do *you* think?"

But the crowd behind her pushed her along, and she didn't get his answer. She suspected he didn't have one, anyway.

Six

At the breakfast table the next morning, Sharon's father read aloud from the newspaper's report on the school board meeting.

" 'Eventually, the police had to forcibly eject members of the audience who refused to leave after the meeting adjourned. A brief struggle ensued between the police and one man who demanded that the school board make a decision on the condom distribution issue immediately.' "

He shook his head, and a crease appeared on his forehead. "I'm glad you two had the good sense to leave when you did."

Sharon picked at her eggs. "I still can't believe the way people were screaming and carrying on."

"Man, I wish I could have been there," Kyle remarked, his eyes bright. "Did anyone try to slug it out?"

"Of course not," Mrs. Delaney said sharply, but she looked concerned, too.

Mr. Delaney was still studying the newspaper

article. "How do the students at Greenwood feel about this, Sharon?"

"I don't know. People haven't been talking about it much." She pushed back her chair. "I guess I'd better start asking, if I'm going to give a report on the show."

As she walked to school, she pondered the events of the evening before. She was still feeling confused by it all. Of course, she'd known there would be arguments. After all, making condoms available in schools was a controversial issue. But she hadn't expected so much emotion, so much passion. Those people were scared. And she had a feeling that it wasn't the threat of disease that had driven them into such a frenzy. It was the idea that their kids might be having sex.

Sex . . . . That's what it was all about. Not condoms, not AIDS. They were worried about teenagers having sex. And Sharon really wanted to know whether or not those parents had reason to be worried.

When she arrived at school, she didn't head toward the regular entrance. There was a courtyard, which could only be entered on one side of the school, and that was her destination. By unwritten law, it was a senior class hangout before and during the school day.

What Sharon hoped was that one of the several seniors she'd worked with on school committees would be there, and would invite her in. Seniors might be able to answer her questions better than juniors. Senior *girls,* preferably, because she wanted to ask some questions she didn't feel quite comfortable asking of boys.

She was in luck. She had just approached the courtyard when she spotted Tanya, a girl she'd spent hours with last spring, making posters for the Thanksgiving canned food drive. Tanya recognized her, and greeted her warmly.

"Hi, Sharon. What's up?"

"I'm working on this new cable TV show," Sharon told her. "Can I ask you some questions?"

"Sure." As they talked, they moved into the courtyard, where groups of seniors were clustered. Tanya drew Sharon over to a corner where two other girls were standing. "Sharon, this is Sarah and Lynn."

"I saw you at Gary Felder's party," Sarah said. "You were with Tyler Ratcliff, right?"

"Lucky you," Lynn commented. "He's a doll."

"Sharon's working on the cable TV show," Tanya told them.

The girls didn't seem to be terribly interested, but Sarah politely asked, "How's it coming along?"

"Okay," Sharon said. She took the plunge. "I'm working on a report about the condom controversy."

That got their full attention. "The what?!" Sarah and Lynn exclaimed in unison.

"You must have heard about it," Sharon said. "There's been a recommendation that high schools distribute condoms to students, to prevent diseases. I went to the school board meeting

90

last night, where they were talking about it. Shouting about it, actually."

"I can believe that," Tanya said. "My parents would have had a fit. I'm sure they think I'm still a virgin."

"Not mine," Lynn said. "At least, not my mother. She fixed me up with birth control pills when I was fourteen."

Sharon couldn't hide her shock. "Fourteen!"

Lynn grinned. "I was mature for my age. And I was a summer camp counselor. *That* gets you off to an early start."

Sharon joined in the laughter, as if she, too, knew from experience what went on among summer camp counselors.

"I was a late bloomer," Sarah told them. "Prom night, last spring."

"Carrying on the old tradition, huh?" Tanya chortled.

"What old tradition?" Sharon asked.

"My sister told me about it," Tanya said. "She's five years older than me. Back when she was here, girls lost their virginity on Prom night. It was like a ritual or something."

"That was the Dark Ages," Lynn noted. "Nowadays, we can't hold out till then."

Sharon's eyes darted among them. "So I guess you guys are in favor of having condoms given out at school."

But just then, the seniors were distracted by the arrival of a couple of boys. It was a good opportunity for Sharon to edge away.

She hadn't gotten the answer to her question.

91

But she'd learned about something else. Something important. If those three girls were typical, then students *were* having sex. And if they were having sex, they needed condoms.

She considered the way they'd talked about having sex, joking and laughing about it. But they're seniors, Sharon thought as she went into the school. It was only natural that they'd be more experienced. She'd have to talk to juniors, maybe even sophomores, to get a more balanced view.

"Sharon!"

"Oh, hi, Tyler."

"You look pretty intense," he noted. "What's up?"

She wasn't about to tell him about the conversation she'd just had. "I was thinking about the school board meeting last night."

"I heard it was pretty wild. My parents were there."

"Yeah?" She looked at him with interest. "How do they stand on the issue?"

"Oh, they're definitely in favor of having condoms available," he assured her.

"Good," Sharon said. "I'm glad they're not freaked out, like some of the parents were last night."

"They're pretty cool, my parents."

"I'd like to meet them."

"You will," Tyler assured her. They'd reached his locker. "We're still on for the football game Friday night, right?"

"Right," Sharon replied, and went down the

hall toward her own locker. Along the way, she saw Kris, leaning against a locker and looking around anxiously.

"Hi," Sharon said. "Waiting for someone?"

Kris spoke so softly Sharon could barely hear her. "Jade. I've made a list of people for her to talk to. I asked her to get some background on the homecoming queen candidates."

"She agreed to help out?" Sharon asked in surprise. "That's great. She seems like such a loner."

"She deserves to be a loner," Kris stated. "She's not even *trying* to fit in here. Who would want to hang out with her?"

"Well, maybe a project like this will help her to meet some people, make friends. See you later, Kris."

Jade might *meet* people, Kris thought, but it wasn't likely that she'd make any friends in the process. Watching Jade approach now, she wondered if there was any point in giving Jade this assignment. Who would talk to *her* about anything?

But she had no other options. So, as soon as Jade came close enough, Kris shoved a sheet of paper at her.

"Here's a list of five girls you should talk to," Kris said. "Now, here are the names of the four candidates: Dana, Tracy, Paula, and Veronica. And these are the girls you should talk to about them." She began to point out the special features of each. "This girl, Brenda, she used to

93

date Veronica's current boyfriend. So I'll bet there are some bad feelings there. And Allison, she didn't make the cheerleading squad. Since Dana was one of the judges, I think—"

"Yeah, yeah, okay." Jade shoved the sheet of paper into her shoulder bag. "Don't worry, I'll get some real garbage." She stalked away.

Kris shuddered. Jade made this sound so *nasty*, so underhanded. I'm only doing this for the good of the school, Kris thought. If one of the girls is doing drugs, or something like that, it would look so bad for Greenwood.

Jade's words didn't inspire confidence. If anything, her attitude served to reinforce the doubts Kris already had. Jade certainly didn't seem to care about Greenwood. It was a puzzle to her, why Jade was suddenly so willing to help out.

But she didn't have time to worry about that now. She had her own job to do. She went to the assistant principal's office, and was pleased to see that Mr. Quimby was in the outer office, talking to the secretary.

"Hello, Mr. Quimby," Kris said brightly. "How are you?"

"Fine, fine," he said, without actually looking at her. "What do you want?"

"I'm working on a report for the new TV show. I was wondering if I could have permission to interview another student during homeroom."

He peered at her suspiciously. "What kind of report? What student?"

She worked up the sweetest smile she was capable of making. "I'm interviewing the homecoming queen candidates for the first program."

He relaxed. "Homecoming queens, eh? Well, that's nice. It's a good topic for the program."

"I think so, too," Kris agreed. "It presents a positive image of Greenwood. I think that's what the program should aim to do." She was kissing up madly to the assistant principal, and it seemed to be working.

He smiled kindly. "I'll give you a homeroom excuse, and a note for you to take to the other student's homeroom."

Armed with her excuses, and the knowledge that she'd scored a few more points with Quimby, Kris hurried to her homeroom where she presented a note to the teacher. Then she went upstairs, to Dana Baldwin's homeroom.

She arranged for the raven-haired girl to be excused, and explained her mission to Dana.

"You want to interview me? On television?"

"Yes," Kris said in a business-like manner. "And I thought it would be a good idea to have a little talk first. Now, let's find an empty room."

They located one, just around the corner. There, Dana sat at a desk and Kris pulled another one around to face her. She pulled a notebook and pen from her handbag.

"Now, let's see . . . . How did you feel when you first learned you were a candidate for homecoming queen?"

"I was thrilled," Dana replied promptly. "Wouldn't any girl be?"

"Absolutely," Kris breathed wistfully. Then

she became businesslike. "Dana, even though we were on the cheerleading squad together, I don't know that much about you. Tell me about yourself."

"I was born right here, in Atlanta," Dana began. As she went on to describe her life, Kris's thoughts drifted. She caught bits and pieces of Dana's autobiography—"ballet lessons until I was twelve," and that sort of thing—but her mind was jumping ahead. When Dana paused to take a breath, she broke in.

"Why do you think you'd be a good homecoming queen?"

The question obviously wasn't one Dana was prepared to answer. She fumbled with her words. "Well, I . . . um . . . I have a lot of school spirit and I like football . . ." She pulled herself together, and the next words came out smoothly. "I think a homecoming queen should be aware that she represents Greenwood High School and present a good image to the community."

She sounds like she's running for Miss America, Kris thought sourly, but her smile remained fixed. "And do you think you'd present a good image?"

Dana considered the question. "I have a B average," she said. "And I'm a cheerleader." She leaned forward. "Kris, I meant to tell you, we all miss you terribly on the squad. I'm so sorry about your accident."

Kris responded with an equally insincere smile. "Thank you. Now, why do you think you'd present a better image than the other candidates?"

"Oh, I wouldn't want to say anything negative about the other girls," Dana protested.

"Of course not," Kris assured her. "And I won't ask you anything like that on TV. But just between us . . ."

Dana bit her lip. "I think a homecoming queen should be a *natural* type of girl."

Kris didn't know what Dana was getting at, but this sounded promising. She nodded to encourage Dana to continue.

"Well, I haven't had a nose job, like *some* people."

Kris's face fell. Lots of people knew Veronica had had a nose job the year before. It wasn't exactly grounds for homecoming queen ineligibility.

Dana spoke conspiratorially. "And you must know about Tracy."

"What about Tracy?"

"She wears a padded bra."

Kris sighed in disappointment. She closed her notebook. "Thanks, Dana."

She'd arranged her next interview in the cafeteria at lunchtime, and met Tracy Egan just as the only junior candidate was sitting down with her lunch tray. Once again, she asked for some background, and again, she half-listened to the girl's recital.

"And I do volunteer work at Dekalb General Hospital," Tracy finished.

"Very interesting," Kris murmured, glancing down at the pad of paper on her lap. It was covered with doodles. "What do you think it takes to be a homecoming queen?"

"I don't think it takes all that much," Tracy said.

Startled, Kris looked up. "Then why would you be any better than anyone else?"

"I wouldn't," Tracy replied promptly. "All a homecoming queen does is wear a crown for a few hours and smile and wave. I think we can all do that pretty well."

This was a total waste of time. Kris knew Tracy. She had no secret past and she wasn't a gossip. And as a junior, Tracy must have known she didn't really have a chance at the crown, so she wouldn't think it was worthwhile criticizing the others or promoting herself.

"How are your grades?" she asked, without much hope.

"As and Bs."

Figures, Kris thought. "Thanks, Tracy."

By the time she met Jade that afternoon, Kris had pretty much dismissed any possibility of seeing a candidate dropped from the list. Veronica Collins had been sweet and bubbly and she absolutely refused to say anything negative about the other girls. Her meeting with Paula was scheduled for the next day, but she didn't anticipate much more from her.

She'd worked hard not to let her jealousy show when she talked to them. It hadn't been easy. These girls seemed to take everything for granted. With all their advantages, they'd never had to struggle the way Kris had. They'd had everything handed to them on a silver platter—ballet lessons, nose jobs, whatever. What had they done to *deserve* this good fortune?

The more Kris thought about that, the more determined she became to find out something, anything, to discredit one of them. But she'd learned nothing.

She wasn't anticipating much from Jade, either. It had been a stupid notion to begin with, Kris decided. What Greenwood girl in her right mind would confide in someone like Jade?

She didn't even expect Jade to show up at the appointed place, by Kris's locker. But Jade was there, leaning against the wall, wearing her usual sullen expression.

Kris got right to the point. "Did you learn anything?"

"Veronica had a nose job."

"I know that," Kris said impatiently. "What else?"

"There was something about Dana and a problem at Rich's."

Kris brightened at the mention of the department store. "Shoplifting?"

"Nah." Jade opened her notebook and looked at a page. "Something about a dress she bought. She wore it to a dance and tried to return it the next day, but the store wouldn't take it back."

"Oh. Well, thanks anyway." Kris turned away to open her locker. She tossed some books in, took one out, and slammed the door shut.

She was surprised to find Jade still there.

"There was one other thing," Jade said slowly.

"I know, I know, Tracy wears a padded bra," Kris replied tiredly.

"No, this is about, what's her name . . ." She consulted her notebook again. "Paula. I heard a rumor about her."

"Paula Skinner?" Kris didn't know her at all, and she could only conjure up a dim image of the girl. "What? She's a Satan worshipper?"

"No. She's pregnant."

Kris drew in her breath sharply. "Are you serious?"

"That's what I heard. From . . ." She checked her notes again. "Layne Farrell."

Kris frowned. Layne was a notorious gossip, and prone to exaggeration. But even so . . .

"Was she sure?" she asked Jade.

Jade shrugged. "All I know is what she told me."

This could be something, Kris thought. *If it's true.* She experienced a pleasant flutter of excitement. "Okay. Thanks, Jade." And this time, she really meant it.

Seven

At 3:30 on Friday afternoon, Sharon went into the old chemistry lab, where the TV show group was meeting again. Debra was already there, holding the folder filled with notes and photocopied articles. Kris and Zack were there, too.

Zack was grumpy. "I hope this meeting doesn't go on too long." When no one echoed his thoughts, his grimace deepened. "Isn't anyone else going to the game tonight?"

"I don't know if I can bear it," Kris said softly.

"Why?" Sharon asked. "You think they're going to lose again?"

"This will be the first game where I won't be cheering," Kris explained. She wiped away an invisible tear. "It will be so painful." She raised her head and gave them all a brave smile. "But I'll go. I have to, to show my support. And to let everyone know that even though I'm not a cheerleader anymore, I still care about the Greenwood Tigers."

"What's *she* running for?" Debra whispered in Sharon's ear.

Sharon shrugged. She was thinking about the football game, too. And Tyler.

As if on cue, Tyler came running in. "Sharon, tell Russell I can't stay for the meeting, okay?"

"What's wrong?" Sharon asked.

"My car's in the shop. I have to get it before they close, or we're not going to have much fun tonight. I'll pick you up at seven, okay?"

"Okay."

He ran out of the room, leaving Sharon to wonder why they couldn't have fun without his car. Did he have plans for activities in the back seat?

She became aware of Zack staring at her. "You're going out with him?"

She nodded. There was something unpleasant in his expression.

"Now I understand why you want condoms at school."

Sharon was appalled. What was wrong with this guy, anyway? One minute he's flirting with her, the next he's being downright nasty. But before she could come back with a snappy retort, Jeff Russell came in.

His normally cheerful expression went sour as he surveyed the group. "Where is everyone?"

"Tyler had to pick up his car," Sharon reported. "It's in the shop."

"What about Jade?"

Nobody knew.

Jeff sighed. "Folks, we go on the air in two

102

weeks. We need to meet regularly, all of us. Kris, how are you coming along on your segment?"

"I've spoken to three of the homecoming queen candidates. They've all agreed to be interviewed."

"What about the fourth?" Jeff asked.

"I was supposed to see her Wednesday, but . . . well, I've had some information I want to check out before I talk to her."

"What kind of information?" Zack asked.

"Oh, just . . . something." A secretive smile played about her lips.

"Have you prepared questions to ask them on TV?" Jeff asked her.

"Oh, sure. Like, 'why do you want to be homecoming queen?' That sort of thing."

Sharon glanced around. Zack was slumped in his chair. Debra's eyes were glazed over. This had to sound as boring to them as it did to her.

The door to the lab opened and Jade came in. She didn't greet the others as she sat down. She didn't offer any explanation or apology for her tardiness, and Jeff didn't ask for any. He simply said, "Jade, try to be on time, okay?" And then he asked, "What have you been doing for the show?"

Jade cast a side-long look at Kris, who answered for her. "She's been doing background work for me. And she's doing a very good job."

Jade spoke. "Did you tell them—"

"Shh," Kris hissed.

Sharon and Debra gave each other puzzled looks at this strange exchange, but Jeff didn't notice anything. He was studying his notes. "Kris, you've got twenty minutes to fill for your segment. Are you going to have enough questions?"

"Oh, sure," Kris said. "In fact, I think this could be a very exciting segment." There was an odd gleam in her eyes that made Sharon wonder if she had plans she wasn't telling them about. But she couldn't ponder that for long. Jeff's attention was on her, now.

"Sharon, what have you prepared?"

"Debra and I have been doing a lot of research, to support the idea of making condoms available through school. I've got statistics on sexually transmitted diseases among adolescents, and on teen pregnancy, too. Then I've got some editorials I can quote from, and I can describe what happened at the school board meeting . . ." Her voice trailed off. No one looked too enthralled with her information.

"I have the same kind of stuff," Zack said. "On the opposite side."

Jeff nodded. "What about student opinion?"

Zack snorted. "My father says student opinion in an issue like this is irrelevant. They don't pay taxes so they don't deserve a voice."

"Nonsense," Jeff snapped. "*All* people are entitled to offer opinions. Sharon, what about you? Do you know how the kids here feel about this issue?"

Sharon shifted uncomfortably in her seat. "It's not easy, talking about a subject like this."

Jeff nodded understandingly. "Maybe you

104

could get student opinions without actually having to talk to them."

"How?"

"Do a survey. People will often write down their true feelings if they know their responses will be anonymous. Does that sound like a good idea to you guys?" His eyes went from Sharon to Zack.

Zack was gazing off into the distance, as if he wasn't even listening. Sharon couldn't picture the former class president handing out surveys. "I'll do it," she said. On a pad of paper, she made a note: 'Compose survey.'

Debra spoke. "Jeff, I don't want to be negative, but I think this show sounds a little, well, not exactly lively."

Jeff wasn't offended. "Have you got any ideas as to how we could liven it up?"

"You mentioned something before about audience participation," Debra said. "Maybe if we gave the audience a chance to ask questions and give their opinions . . ."

"You're assuming we'll *get* an audience," Zack broke in. "I don't think there's enough interest in this show to get people to watch it being taped."

"Maybe that's because we don't have a name yet," Kris piped up. "I've come up with an idea for a title."

"Let's hear it," Jeff said.

" 'The Happy Hour.' "

Zack shook his head. "It sounds like a bar."

"Besides," Sharon said, "It's not accurate. We won't just be talking about 'happy' subjects."

Zack leaned forward. "If we want this show to be taken seriously, we need a serious name. Something like 'Contemporary Discussion.'"

"That's awful," Debra said bluntly. "It sounds like one of those boring Sunday morning political shows."

Jeff's expression was impassive. "Jade? We haven't heard from you. Is there some sort of modern expression you can think of, some slang or phrase that suggests meeting problems in a straightforward way?"

"Why are you asking me?" Jade demanded to know.

Jeff countered with, "Why not? You're a member of this group, aren't you?"

Jade scowled. "How about . . . 'In Your Face'?"

Kris shuddered. "That sounds awfully . . ." She struggled for a word.

"Hostile," Debra supplied.

Jeff ran his fingers through his hair. "We need to come to some sort of general consensus about a title, and fast. I want you all to think about this. We'll have another meeting on Tuesday after class. Everyone should come with at least one good idea for a name. Okay?"

The nods and "okays" weren't exactly enthusiastic. Sharon thought Jeff was beginning to look a little nervous. She couldn't blame him.

The evenings were getting a little bit cooler. For the football game, Sharon debated wearing her new long denim skirt, but she decided it

106

would be difficult climbing the bleachers in it. She exchanged it for jeans, black ones, and a short-sleeved ribbed jersey. But once she had the top on, she wondered if the neckline was a bit too deep. She didn't want Tyler to get the idea she was trying to look sexy . . .

Or did she? Her thoughts went back to the party last Saturday night. With a little concentration, she could relive the sensations she'd felt before she'd pushed him away.

When he'd held her, kissed her, in that TV room, she'd felt nice. More than nice. But confused, too. She'd wanted him to continue. And she'd wanted him to stop. How would she feel if—when—anything happened tonight? Would there still be that confusion? Or would she know what to do?

"Face it, Sharon," she said aloud. "You don't know *what* you want."

Her stomach was growling, but she didn't want to eat anything. They'd be going out after the game, for burgers or pizza or something. And after that . . . she shook her head vigorously, as if she was trying to forcibly eject the possibilities from lingering in her mind.

She checked the clock on her bedside table, and saw that she had a half-hour to kill before Tyler came to get her. Her parents had gone out to dinner, and Kyle was at a friend's. She needed something to do, to keep her uncertainties at bay.

Resolutely, she sat down at her desk and opened a textbook. Seconds later, she closed it. Homework wouldn't distract her. She remembered the survey Jeff had suggested she conduct. She decided to start on that now.

She turned on her word processor, and began typing. "Survey for Greenwood High students. All answers will be confidential." Then she created blanks for the students to fill in their age, class, and sex. It would be interesting to see how the opinions varied between the sexes and the classes.

The first question was easy. "#1. Do you believe condoms should be made available without charge in the health clinic?" She double-spaced, and typed "#2." Then her hands froze above the keyboard. What else was there to ask? This one question would give her all the information she needed.

It seemed silly to pass out a survey with only one question on it. Maybe she should take advantage of this opportunity to learn the answers to some other questions.

But her hands didn't move. Was this legitimate, she wondered, using the survey to satisfy her own curiosity? She stared at the screen for a while. Surely, she could justify asking more questions. It was all related, in a way.

She began typing again. "Have you ever had sexual relations? How old were you when you first had sexual relations?" She bit her lip. Then, with grim determination, she typed, "How long would you go out with someone before having sexual relations?"

She got so involved with her work that it took her a minute before her brain registered the fact that the doorbell was ringing. She left the desk and ran downstairs.

"Hi. How's your car?"

"It's moving," Tyler said, coming inside. "I guess that's all I can hope for."

"I'm ready to leave," Sharon told him. "I just have to get my purse." She started back toward the stairs.

"Can I come up with you?" Tyler asked. "I've never seen the upstairs."

His face was perfectly innocent. But all Sharon could think of was that upstairs there were bedrooms, and in bedrooms there were beds—and that no one else was home. And she remembered the survey, still up on the computer screen.

"Actually, I don't really need my purse, do I?"

"What about your keys?"

"My parents will be here when I get home. And I've got some money in my pocket. Let's go. We don't want to miss the kick-off."

On the short ride to Greenwood, Sharon filled him in on the meeting he'd missed. "Everytime Zack opens his mouth, he quotes his father. Doesn't he have any opinions of his own?"

"Maybe he's scared to have any," Tyler commented. "Poor guy."

"I guess I'd be more sympathetic if he didn't always make nasty cracks."

"What did he say?" Tyler asked.

Sharon opened her mouth, and then snapped it shut. No way was she going to relate Zack's comment on why Sharon wanted condoms made available at school. "Oh, he's just generally unpleasant to me."

"He's got a strange attitude toward girls," Tyler said. "I've heard him talking in the locker room, bragging about his conquests and all that."

"With *who*? I've never noticed him hanging around with any particular girl at school."

"He claims the girls he dates go to Woodside Girls' Academy. I have a feeling his stories are figments of his imagination. If not, Woodside's entire student body looks like a combination of Michelle Pfieffer and Kim Basinger. And they're all *completely* subservient." He shook his head. "He's got a real dark ages mentality, very macho and sexist. He doesn't like assertive women. That's probably why he's not very nice to you."

Sharon glanced at him curiously. "You think I'm assertive?"

"Sure. Don't you want to be?"

"Of course, but . . . Debra says sometimes I'm pushy."

Tyler laughed. "That's not the word I'd use. Of course, we don't know each other all that well yet, do we?"

"No, we don't. But—"

"We will," Tyler said. Then he groaned. "Oh, no, now *I* sound pushy."

"No, you don't," Sharon said quickly. "But what I wanted to say is that, if you ever think I'm acting pushy, like at the TV meetings, I want you to tell me."

He stopped at a red light and looked at her.

"And if you ever think I'm behaving badly, you tell me, okay?"

She nodded.

"Sharon . . ." He hesitated, and then plunged in. "Maybe you'll think I'm a jerk for talking like this. But ever since we met, I've had this feeling we were meant to be together. I've never had the kind of relationship I'd like to have with a girl. A totally honest relationship. Where we wouldn't make each other crazy trying to figure each other out. We'd talk, and share, and let our real feelings show. I think . . . I hope we can have that. What do you think?"

"That's what I want, too," Sharon said with real feeling. "With you."

His anxious face took on hope, and his sudden smile exuded warmth and gratitude. "The only reason I came to that *News* meeting was to get closer to you. It's why I joined the TV group, too." He grinned ruefully. "Jeff Russell's bound to figure that out pretty soon. I don't know what I'm actually going to *do* on this show. I'm no good at debate, and I don't really want to do research." He pulled into the parking lot and took the car into a space. Turning off the motor, he sat still for a moment. "I didn't care about it when I signed up. But now I feel like a fraud."

Sharon touched his arm. "You're no fraud. You're the most real person I've ever met."

Tyler smiled. They got out of the car and he took Sharon's hand. "You're terrific, Sharon."

She *felt* terrific. And like magic, those fears and concerns that had been nagging her earlier in the evening faded away. Hearing him express himself like that, exposing his own vulnerability, his insecurity, made her feel closer to him than ever. So many guys she knew would never admit to feeling less than confident about anything. Tyler was special. She'd suspected that before, but now she knew for sure. She squeezed his hand, and they hurried off to the stadium.

It was a good game. Greenwood hadn't had a winning team for several years, and they'd lost the first two games of the season. But tonight, either the Tigers were getting it together, or the other team was really lame. In any case, Greenwood looked good on the field.

During the slower moments in the game and the time-outs, she and Tyler chatted with friends and classmates sitting around them. Several times, Sharon caught admiring glances from girls cast their way. They envy me, she realized. And they had a *right* to be envious. How many guys at Greenwood were as good-looking, bright, and sensitive as Tyler? I'm a lucky girl, Sharon thought.

The Tigers won the game by a narrow margin, and the crowd went wild. Over the cheers, Tyler yelled, "How about something to eat?"

"Great!" Sharon screamed back.

Unfortunately, it appeared that the entire stadium had the same idea. They headed for a small popular restaurant, across from the Emory University campus. Tyler had to circle the area three times before they found a parking place. Once they got out of the car, they could see the place was packed.

"Look at the wait for tables," Tyler complained. "And I'm starving."

"I've got an idea," Sharon said. "Why don't we get food to go, and we'll find someplace to eat on campus."

"You're a genius," Tyler stated. "Cheeseburgers and fries?" He charged into the restaurant.

Sharon waited happily outside. It was a lovely night, still warm, but not muggy, with just a hint of an autumn breeze.

Tyler emerged moments later, holding the bags high in triumph.

"How did you do that so fast?" Sharon asked.

"I walked in, and the crowd parted like the Red Sea," he declared grandly.

"Oh, *really?*" Sharon gave him an exaggerated look of awe. "My goodness, I had no idea you were so famous."

He grinned. "I've got connections. My cousin works behind the counter. C'mon, let's find a place to eat."

They crossed the road and entered the university campus. Ultimately, they located a bench in a pretty corner of a deserted quadrangle.

"I've been thinking about the TV program," Sharon said, as they unwrapped their burgers and fries. "You should talk to Jeff about it. Maybe he'll come up with an idea for something you can do."

Tyler poked a straw through the plastic top of his soda. "Like what?"

"I don't know. What do you *want* to do?"

Tyler shrugged. "That's what my parents are always asking me. I wish I knew."

Sharon knew he wasn't referring to the TV show now. "You mean, what you're going to do after graduation?"

He nodded. "I've applied to Georgia Tech. It's where my father went, and he really wants me to go there. But . . . I don't want to be an engineer, Sharon. I want to be involved with music."

"Did you tell your parents that?"

"Yeah. They think music is a great hobby, but they don't think it's a practical career choice."

Sharon dipped her french fry into the little pool of ketchup they'd made on a napkin. "Tyler, tell me more about your music."

"It's hard to talk about," he said. "I'm trying to come up with a certain sound, something personal but something people can relate to. My songs . . . they're about why people do what they do, the feelings that drive them into one action or another. Does that make sense?"

Sharon was about to say "sure" but she remembered what they'd talked about earlier. Honesty. "I think I'd understand better if I heard your music."

"You will," Tyler promised. "This week." He studied his hamburger. "I've got songs I've never played and sang for anyone. I want you to hear them. Only you."

"Really?"

"Really."

They both fell silent. Then it seemed only

natural to push the food aside and fall into each other's arms.

It was the longest kiss they'd ever shared. Those warm, cozy feelings enveloped Sharon again, drawing her closer and tighter to him. Those feelings were followed by a tingly sensation, an awareness of every nerve in her body responding to his touch. They clung to each other, touching and stroking. She felt an overwhelming need, a huge desire to be a part of him, and she sensed the same need in him. They seemed in rhythm, like one being, united . . .

Then there was panic. "No. Tyler, stop."

"We can't stop," he whispered.

"Tyler! No!" With force, she pushed him away.

Her action took him by surprise. And then he was angry. "What's the matter with you?"

"Me? You're the one who . . . who—"

"Who what? Who wants to be close? You want it, too! Are you going to tell me you don't?"

She couldn't answer that. She was shaking, all over. Somehow, she managed to get to her feet. "I want to go home. I mean, *have* to go home."

"Why?"

"Because—because I don't have keys. My parents go to bed early."

He clutched his head. "Sharon, you're making me crazy. Look, we've got something special happening. I . . . I think I love you. And I think you think you love me, too. Am I right?"

Dumbly, she nodded.

"Then why can't we be together? Why can't we—"

"Because!" she cried out. "Because . . . I have to go home."

The bewilderment left his face and was replaced by . . . nothing. Stiffly, like a robot, he began picking up the remnants of their dinner, and threw them in a nearby trash can.

Despite the warm night air, Sharon shivered and hugged herself while she waited. In silence, they walked off the campus and back to where the car was parked. They remained silent all the way home.

He pulled into her driveway. But he didn't turn off the motor, and neither of them moved. She broke the silence.

"I'm sorry." It wasn't what she wanted to say, but it was all she could think of.

"Don't be sorry," he said. "Just talk to me. Tell me what's going on. I don't understand."

But she couldn't do that. Because she didn't know what to say, and she didn't understand either.

"Do you want to get together again?" he asked.

She was surprised at how fast she was able to respond. "Yes. I want to know you better, Tyler. I want to hear your music. I want . . ." Her voice trailed off.

"Okay." He turned off the engine, they both got out, and he walked her to the door.

They stood there awkwardly. "I want to kiss you," he said. "Kiss me," she said urgently. He did.

And it only made everything more confusing.

Eight

On Monday morning, practically feverish with excitement, Kris waited outside Paula's homeroom. She still wasn't sure how she would discover the truth about Paula's condition. You couldn't just come right out and ask someone, "Excuse me, but are you pregnant?"

She conjured up a picture of the girl who she'd only seen in passing, at school dances and other events. She was very pretty, Kris recalled, slender with long dark hair and a pale complexion. Her eyes searched the hall for this person.

Finally, she spotted her, walking alone and rapidly. She didn't notice Kris waving at her, and she didn't slow down as she approached, but kept walking, past Kris and down the hall.

Kris followed her. Paula turned the corner and went into the seldom used restroom, the one where Kris had met Jade. Kris went in after her.

Paula had already gone into a cubicle, and Kris heard the unmistakable sounds of someone being sick. A moment later, a wan Paula came out of the cubicle and went to a sink. She splashed some water on her face.

"Paula?"

She looked up, her face devoid of color. "Yes?"

"I'm Kris. I called you about being on the cable TV show."

"Oh, right. Sorry about . . ." She gestured vaguely toward the cubicle. "I've been getting these upset stomachs."

"Oh, really?" Kris offered a politely sympathetic smile which she hoped masked her intense interest.

"Mm." Paula's own smile was tired. "Now, you said you wanted to interview all the homecoming queen candidates on the TV show, right?"

"Yes, that's the idea. But I wanted to meet with each of you first, to get some background information. Can you tell me anything about your hobbies, your attitudes, your recent activities?"

"Hobbies, huh? Well, I do some embroidery. And I've been taking piano for years. I'm not very good at it, though."

"That's interesting," Kris murmured, scribbling doodles on her pad. "Do you have a boyfriend?"

"Yes. But I wouldn't call him a hobby!"

"A *serious* boyfriend?" Her eyes were on Paula's stomach.

Paula gazed at her curiously. "Why are you so interested in my boyfriend?"

"Well, I just wondered if he was someone on the football team."

"No. He doesn't go to Greenwood." Paula took

a makeup kit out of her purse. From the kit, she extracted a compact and began applying blush. "It's a pain, not having any mirrors in here," she commented.

"Yeah. Paula, since the homecoming queen represents Greenwood High, do you think you'd present a good image?"

"I think I'm pretty typical, if that's what you mean."

"Oh, *really*?"

Paula closed the compact case with a sharp snap. "What's *that* supposed to mean?"

"Huh?"

"You keep saying, 'oh, really,' like I'm lying to you. What's your problem? What are you getting at?"

This direct question caught Kris off guard. It took her a second to remember who was the bad girl here. She faced Paula squarely. "It's just that I've heard something . . ."

"What have you heard?" Paula asked. She didn't look fearful. If anything, her expression was defiant.

"That . . . that . . ." Kris tossed all attempts at tact aside. "That you're pregnant."

"What does that have to do with being a candidate for homecoming queen?"

Kris gasped. She had expected a denial, a show of surprise. "You mean, you *are*?"

"Yes." Paula threw the makeup bag into her purse. "Anything else you need to know?"

Kris was speechless.

"See you on TV," Paula said. She was at the door before Kris recovered her wits.

"Wait! What are you going to do about it?"

"About what?"

"Being pregnant."

Paula smiled slightly. "I guess I'm going to have a baby." With that, she left the restroom.

Kris was wondering if she'd heard correctly. Paula wasn't trying to keep it a secret! There were no tears, no pleas for Kris to keep this to herself. Paula wasn't even *ashamed!* If it was her, Kris, who was pregnant, she'd want to die. She'd crawl in a hole to hide, forever!

She hurried out of the restroom and went directly to her own homeroom. There, she found three friends already gathered. Now she could find out if others found this situation as shocking as she did. She sat down and pulled her chair closer to them. "Wait till you guys hear this," she announced. "I've got the story of the century."

Her friends lit up and began pushing their desks closer toward hers. "What's up?" Beth Ann asked.

For one split second, Kris hesitated. She was about to ruin a girl's reputation. But no, Paula had done that to herself. People were bound to find out, sooner or later. And why shouldn't they find out *before* the homecoming queen elections?

No, there was no reason to feel guilty about spreading this news. Speaking softly and slowly, with expression and dramatic gestures, she told her story. Their reactions were gratifying.

"Pregnant!" Lori drew in her breath with a sharp hissing sound. "Wow."

Beth Ann's eyes doubled in size. "She's going to have the baby?"

"That's what she said."

"And I always thought she was a *nice* girl," Lori said.

Molly appeared less shocked than the others. "It happens, I guess. Remember Kelly Howard? *She* was nice."

"But she wasn't a candidate for homecoming queen," Kris said. "Guys, do you realize what this means?"

"What if she wins?" Beth Ann mused. "How will it make Greenwood look, to have a pregnant homecoming queen?"

"It would make us all look like tramps," Kris declared hotly.

"You're right," Lori agreed, shuddering. "We'll be the joke of Atlanta."

"But she *won't* win," Kris said. "I'm going to make her admit being pregnant. Right on TV. I'm going to ask her—"

"Wait a minute," Holly interrupted. "When is this TV show happening?"

"We're taping it a week from Thursday."

"We vote the day after that," Holly said. "Personally, no offense, Kris, I don't think a lot of kids will be seeing the show. And the word about Paula won't have spread by the next day."

Kris sank back in her chair. She hadn't considered that.

"And she's awfully popular," Beth Ann noted.

"Even if people heard the rumor, they might vote for her anyway."

Kris's brain was working overtime. "Maybe not. They can't vote for her if she's not on the ballot."

"You think she'll drop out of the running?" Lori asked.

"She won't have to," Kris said. She looked up at the clock. The bell would be ringing soon. She got up and went to the teacher's desk.

"Could I be excused to go see Mr. Quimby? It's urgent."

"Sharon!"

Sharon paused and waited in the hall for Debra to catch up with her.

"Where are you going?" Debra asked. "The bell's about to ring."

"I've got an excuse. I have to go photocopy the survey. If I'm going to have results before the show, the surveys have to get distributed today."

"Can I see it?"

Sharon handed her the neatly typed survey. As Debra read it, her eyebrows practically met her hairline.

"Wow, this is pretty personal stuff. You really need to ask all these questions about people's sex lives?"

"Shh," Sharon said. She lowered her voice. "Hey, you were the one who wanted me to find out if people at Greenwood really needed condoms."

"And you'll probably get more honest answers with a written survey."

Sharon agreed. "Right. And it won't be so embarrassing. I'm going to leave these in a box by the front door, with a sign. People can put the surveys back in the box after they've filled them out."

"Good idea," Debra said. "Hey, how was your date with Tyler, Friday?"

"Fine," Sharon said quickly. "Look, I'd better run. There might be a wait for the photocopy machine."

She took off, aware that her heartbeat had quickened at the very mention of Tyler's name. She hadn't seen him since Friday night. Several times, on Saturday and Sunday, she'd found herself wishing he would call. She'd considered calling him, too. But she hadn't, and she was almost glad *he* hadn't, either. She wouldn't have known what to say. How could she explain her feelings when she didn't understand them herself?

This survey would help her, she thought. Through the answers, she would learn how other girls were dealing with this issue. Maybe after reading the survey results, she could figure out what she was supposed to do, how she was supposed to feel.

Luckily, the photocopy machine was free. She filled out the necessary forms with the secretary, indicating that this was for a school activity. She was placing the survey face down on the screen when Tyler came in.

"Hi," he said. "I was passing by when I saw you in here. So I thought I'd stop and say . . . hi."

"That's nice." She busied herself punching buttons on the photocopy machine, glad to have an excuse not to meet his eyes as she greeted him.

"How's it going?" he asked casually.

"Fine," she replied. She noticed that a light on the machine was blinking. "Excuse me." She went back to the secretary. "I think the machine needs toner."

The secretary gave her a look that suggested Sharon had personally sabotaged the machine, but she went to the closet and got the toner. Just then, the bell rang, but Tyler didn't take off.

"Don't you have to be in homeroom?" Sharon asked.

"I have a note. I've just been to see Jeff Russell about the show."

"What did he say?"

"I told him I didn't think there was anything I could do for this TV show."

Stricken, Sharon finally faced him directly. "You mean, you're quitting the group?"

"Oh, I'm sticking with it," he assured her. "But I've got a different job. I'm going to be the announcer."

Sharon clapped her hands. "Tyler, that's fantastic!"

He nodded happily. "Yeah, it's perfect for me. I get to introduce the speakers and the stories, and maybe run around the audience with a microphone, taking questions."

Sharon laughed. "Greenwood's own Phil Donahue!"

Tyler clutched his head. "I hope they don't make me cut my hair."

"No way," Sharon proclaimed. "I won't let them." Their eyes locked. Suddenly, it was as if the Friday night conflict had never happened.

"Machine's ready," the secretary announced.

"Thanks." Sharon punched in some numbers and hit start.

"What's that?" Tyler asked.

"A survey. Jeff suggested I get student opinion on . . . my segment." Why was she suddenly having a hard time saying the word 'condom?' It had never bothered her before.

"Can I see it?" Tyler asked.

She couldn't say no. And what would be the point? He could always pick up a copy later in the day, and he'd know she'd composed it.

Silently, she took one of the copies from the tray and handed it to him. She couldn't watch his expression while he read it, and so she stared at the sheets tumbling into the tray.

"Did you write these questions?" he asked after a moment.

"Yes." She forced herself to face him. She couldn't read his expression. And before either of them could say anything more, Mr. Quimby came out of his office and approached the machine.

"Are you finished with this?" he barked.

"Yes, sir." Sharon scooped up the copies in her arms. One sheet floated to the floor.

Mr. Quimby picked it up. With trepidation, Sharon watched as he perused the survey. Her

125

worry turned to outright fear as she saw an angry redness come into his face.

"What sort of garbage is this?" he bellowed.

Sharon struggled to keep her voice steady. "It's a survey, to gather information for a segment on the cable TV show."

Now Quimby was practically purple. "What kind of segment?"

Sharon sensed Tyler moving in closer, as if in a show of support. She wished she could take his hand and feel that support. But this was *her* problem, and she had to stand on her own.

She spoke calmly and deliberately. "The subject is whether or not condoms should be freely distributed in high schools. I'm trying to find out how sexually active the students at Greenwood are, so I can make a recommendation—"

He interrupted with an expression of disbelief. "So *you* can make a recommendation? What business is this of yours?"

Tyler jumped in. "She's a student here. This is every student's business."

Mr. Quimby waved the paper in the air. "And Mr. Russell is aware of this?"

Sharon was about to explain that Jeff hadn't seen the actual survey, but before she could, Kris burst into the office.

"Mr. Quimby, I need to talk to you."

"Not now," the assistant principal said irritably, but Kris persisted.

"It's serious, Mr. Quimby. *Very* serious." The urgency in her voice couldn't be ignored.

"All right, all right," Quimby growled. But he

126

pointed a stern finger at Sharon. "We're not finished, young lady. You run along to class, but I'm planning to talk to Mr. Russell."

He marched back to his office, and Kris followed.

Sharon was still clutching her surveys, and she noticed that the knuckles on her hands were white. "Thank you, Kris," she whispered.

"Yeah, that was good timing," Tyler said. "She got him flustered. I think he was about to forbid you from passing out those surveys."

"But he didn't," Sharon said. With determination, she added, "These surveys are going to be right by the door, where everyone can see them."

"Good," Tyler declared. "That was great, the way you stood up to him. You're one tough lady, Sharon."

She could see that he meant it as a compliment. She grinned. "I guess sometimes, being pushy is a virtue." She looked down at the surveys. "I'm going to make a sign and find a box for these."

"I'll give you a hand," Tyler said.

He meant that literally, too. And Sharon happily took it.

Sitting behind his desk, Mr. Quimby's color showed a remarkable range. It had gone from purple all the way to red. And as Kris reported her news, his face turned practically white.

"You're sure of this?" he asked.

"That's what she told me," Kris replied.

Mr. Quimby picked up his phone, punched a button, and spoke to the secretary. "Locate Paula Skinner and send her to my office immediately."

Nine

Throughout the morning, Sharon thought about Mr. Quimby's anger over her survey. The more she relived the experience, the more worried she became. She wasn't that concerned for herself. The worst Quimby could do would be to locate the box of surveys by the school exit and remove them.

It was Jeff Russell who occupied her mind. He was the TV show advisor, and Quimby was going to hold him responsible.

She had Jeff Russell for English third period. The instant that the bell rang at the end of second period, she shot out of the classroom, raced down the hall, and up the stairs. She wanted to tell him about the survey before he saw it, and warn him about Quimby's reaction.

She was too late. Sitting at his desk in the still empty classroom, Jeff Russell was studying the survey when Sharon ran in. Nervously, she approached his desk.

He was so engrossed in his reading that he

didn't notice her right away. "Mr. Russell?" she said tentatively.

It was a relief when he looked up and smiled. "Hello, Sharon." There was no anger or distress in his greeting. Still, Sharon felt compelled to offer an apology. "I'm sorry I didn't show the survey to you, first."

To her surprise, Jeff shook his head. "There was no need for you to do that. The students are in charge of this show. You don't have to submit everything to me for approval." Then his lips twitched. "Of course, you could have asked for my advice, if you'd wanted to."

Sharon bowed her head humbly. "If I'd showed this to you, what kind of advice would you have given me?"

Now he gave her a full smile. "I would have said exactly what I'm going to say now. It's an excellent survey, Sharon. True, it goes beyond the issue of condom distribution, but that's okay. Maybe we need to extend this subject. These questions could lead us into another direction we should explore. We might learn something very important from this survey."

Yes, please, Sharon thought fervently. *Let me learn something very important. Something that will tell me what to do about Tyler!*

Other students were coming in now, and a couple of them approached the desk to speak to Mr. Russell. But Sharon still had one more question she needed to ask the teacher, to ease her mind. "Mr. Quimby saw the survey, and he wasn't too happy about it. Did he—"

"Yes, we had a brief meeting," the teacher told her. "But you've got nothing to worry about. You see, according to the conditions of the grant that's paying for this show, the students involved are guaranteed freedom of expression. There are no restrictions on subject matter. As for the surveys . . . no one's forcing students to fill them out, right?"

Sharon gazed at him in open admiration. She wanted to let him know how much she appreciated his support, but the students waiting to see him were closing in.

"Thank you," she said, and moved away, allowing other students to talk to him. It's all going to be okay, she thought as she took her seat. Students would be able to fill out the forms, and she'd get all the information she needed. For the show . . . and for herself.

She had phys ed after English. In the locker room, changing her clothes, she greeted Andie McKay, who had the locker next to hers.

"Hi," Andie responded, tossing her books and handbag into the locker. But Sharon saw that she didn't take out her gym clothes before closing it.

"You're not playing basketball?" Sharon asked.

"I've got cramps," Andie told her with a grimace.

"Oh, too bad," Sharon murmured sympathetically.

"It's okay," Andie said. "Actually, I should be celebrating. I was almost two weeks late this month, and I was totally freaking out."

Beth Ann, who also had a locker in that row,

overheard them talking. "Boy, do I know that feeling."

"You do?" Sharon asked in surprise, remembering their conversation at Gary Felder's party. "I thought you were on—" she stopped suddenly, thinking that maybe Beth Ann might not want the whole world to know how she avoided pregnancy.

But Beth Ann didn't have any problem with that. "I don't always remember to take the pill every day. Believe me, I've had some close calls."

"*I* should get on the pill," Andie remarked casually. "It would certainly give me peace of mind."

"But don't you use condoms?" Sharon asked. "I mean, there's not just pregnancy to worry about."

"Yeah, I know," Andie said. "But sometimes, it's just not convenient, you know what I mean?"

Another girl, Dinah, joined them. "What *are* you guys talking about?"

"Condoms," Andie told her. "Sometimes a guy just doesn't have any on him and all the stores are closed. And some guys *hate* using them."

"Well, I carry my own," Dinah said. "And if a guy doesn't like to use them, that's just too bad. I just say, 'hey man, no glove, no love.' "

Other girls were gathering around them. "Condoms take all the romance out of making love," one of them complained.

Another girl laughed. "Once I went into a drugstore to buy some. And right behind me in

132

line was this friend of my parents! I ended up buying cough drops instead."

Now they were all laughing and exchanging anecdotes about buying condoms, or not using condoms. Sharon hoped her fixed smile covered any sign of the discomfort she felt. They all sounded so casual, so nonchalant, like having sex was no more significant than brushing your teeth.

It was a relief to get into the gym and onto the basketball court, where no one would be talking about sex. But there seemed to be no place where she could escape from the subject that particular day. Right in the middle of a time-out, when they were supposed to be discussing team strategy, someone mentioned a new boy at school. "He's only a sophomore, but have you checked him out? Seriously gorgeous."

"Not too bright, though," another girl said. "I heard he was held back at his old school."

"So what?" the first speaker countered. "I'm not saying I want to marry him. I just want to jump his bones!"

Raucous, knowing laughter greeted her comment. Sharon laughed, too. But at the same time, she was trying to remember if this had always been a common topic at school. Maybe it had been, and she just hadn't been paying attention.

She was paying attention, now. At lunchtime, she joined a group of girls she often sat with in the cafeteria. Sonya, a vivacious girl who Sharon had known since elementary school, was flapping a sheet of paper in the air. "Have y'all seen this? It's a *sex* survey!"

Sharon thought she did a pretty good job of imitating the surprise and curiosity of the other girls.

"Who's giving it out?" Sandra asked.

"I don't know," Sonya replied. "There's no name on it. Oh, wait, it says 'this survey is strictly confidential, for use by the Greenwood High School cable television program. All responses will be anonymous.' "

"What kind of questions are there?" Dinah asked, peering over Sonya's shoulder. She read aloud. " 'How old were you when you first had sexual relations?' "

Sonya smiled. "I think I was . . . fifteen. Yes, that's right. In fact, it was after the homecoming game last year. Gee, do you realize what that means? Pretty soon, I'll have my first anniversary!"

"First anniversary of what?" Sharon asked.

Sonya struck a pose. "Of becoming a real woman!"

"I can't even remember my first time," Dinah said loftily. "It's been too long."

"I can," Sandra said, smiling dreamily. "It was the summer I visited my cousin in California. He was an older guy, at least eighteen."

"Cute?" Dinah asked.

"Unbelievably. He was an actor. Mostly in commercials, but I swear, I think I saw him on 'Beverly Hills 90210' last month. In a crowd scene."

"How old were you?" Sharon asked.

Sandra studied her fingernails. "Thirteen."

Sharon choked back a gasp. She looked around. None of the other girls looked the least bit fazed.

"I was thirteen when I started fooling around," Dinah reported. "But I didn't go all the way. I waited at least a year before that."

Then they were all exchanging the stories of their first times. Sharon, still retaining her fixed smile, sat back in her chair and pondered the conversation. She *knew* these girls. They'd gone to school together for years. Where had she been when all this was going on?

Then they started talking about condoms. "It would be nice to get them for free," Sonya said, examining the survey. "They're not cheap."

"But I'd feel funny," Sandra noted, "asking the clinic nurse for them."

"I think the guys should be responsible for getting condoms," Dinah said decisively.

"But what if they won't?" Sandra inquired. "We have to take care of ourselves. Sonya, what do you think?"

Sonya was the only one among them with a serious boyfriend. "Pete and I don't use them." She leaned forward and lowered her voice. "We've only ever been with each other. Don't repeat that, okay? I don't mind if people know that he was my first. I mean, we've been going together for two years. But if the other guys found out I was his first—"

"They'd tease him big time," Dinah stated.

"Exactly," Sonya affirmed. "People expect guys

to be more experienced. Sharon, what about you and Tyler?"

Sharon gulped. "What about us?"

"Are you using condoms?"

"You'd better be," Sandra said. "No offense, but I'm sure you're not Tyler's first. After all, he's a senior, and very cute."

"You *are* being careful, aren't you?" Dinah asked.

Sharon's head was spinning. She couldn't answer that.

"Are you okay?" Sonya asked. Then her eyes narrowed. "Oh, I get it. You and Tyler haven't done it yet."

Sharon didn't answer that either, but Dinah was already shaking her head reproachfully. "How many times have you gone out with him?"

"We've had three dates," Sharon said. Her face was getting hot.

"And you two haven't—"

"I didn't say that," Sharon interrupted.

Sandra grinned. "That's what I figured. Guys don't stick around if girls don't . . . well, show that they care. They don't have a lot of patience. If a girl isn't interested, they give up pretty fast, y'know?"

"Right," the others agreed.

"I know," Sharon said faintly.

Sonya was looking at her curiously. "Are you sure you're okay, Sharon? You look sort of out of it."

"I'm okay," Sharon responded automatically.

"I've got a lot on my mind." She pushed back her chair.

"You haven't eaten your lunch," Dinah noted.

"I'm not hungry. And I have to . . . uh, I have to go to the media center."

As she walked through the cafeteria, Sharon looked at every girl she passed. The same question hung over her head. How many sexual experiences had they had? She was beginning to wonder if she was the only girl—except for Debra—who hadn't had *any*.

It dawned on her that she didn't even need to see the results of her survey. She knew already that she was one of the only girls at Greenwood who had never had intimate relations with a guy. She was a freak. Anyone looking at her could probably see that she was nowhere near becoming a woman.

And it was just her luck that she *would* have to run into Tyler, right at that moment, when she was feeling so utterly pathetic.

She ducked her head. The way she was feeling, she probably had virgin with a capital "v" written all over her.

But he was calling to her, and she couldn't ignore him. She managed a half-smile as he came near. "Hi, Tyler."

"I just checked," he said, "and the box with the surveys is still by the door. So it looks like Quimby isn't going to confiscate them."

"Mr. Russell says it's completely legit," Sharon told him. "I just hope kids pick them up."

"I saw some guys in my last class filling them out," Tyler announced.

"That's good."

"Yeah. I just hope they tell the truth."

"What do you mean?" Sharon asked. "Why wouldn't they? The surveys are anonymous."

Tyler shrugged. "Well, you know how it is. If they fill them out in front of other guys, they might exaggerate."

"Really?"

"Sure," Tyler said, and grinned. "Some guys are jerks. They want to show off, that sort of thing."

"Oh."

"Anyway," Tyler continued, "when you get the surveys back, I wouldn't mind going over them with you."

Oh, sure, Sharon thought. *I'm going to let you see how weird I really am. An oddity, a weirdo, a freak. The most immature girl in the entire junior class. Little Miss Purity and Chastity.* She gave him a noncommittal nod. "I have to go to the media center. See ya'."

"Sharon, wait."

She turned back.

"Saturday night?"

"What about it?" she asked.

"You want to go out? Catch a movie . . . or maybe I could play you some music?"

Her heart was full. He wasn't giving up, she thought. She was aware of conflicting emotions colliding in her head. She could say no. Nicely, of course, and with a good excuse—family plans, or something like that. Then, if he asked her out for another night, she could say no again, with another fabricated excuse. The excuses would start getting flimsy, he'd get the message, and stop asking. It would be over, and there'd be no more decisions for her to make.

All that raced through her mind as he stood there, waiting for a reply. I can say no, she assured herself. It's a very easy thing to say. But there was one small problem. She didn't want to say no.

"All right. Saturday."

"Great," he said. "See ya' later."

She floated out of the cafeteria, basking in the wave of that happy smile he'd left her with, and without a thought for what she would have to face this weekend.

Vaguely, as she went down the hall, she heard someone call her name.

"Hey, space to Sharon, come in, Sharon," Debra intoned. "Are you there?"

Sharon gathered her wits. "Of course I'm here."

"Well, you look like you're in another world," Debra remarked. "What's up? Did you just have a magic moment with Tyler? I saw him go into the cafeteria."

Sharon brushed that aside. "I was thinking about the TV show. In fact, I'm glad I ran into you. We need to pull all that research together, so I can give a decent report at the meeting tomorrow. Can you come over after school?"

"Sure," Debra said promptly. "But that is *not* what you were thinking about."

Sharon continued to ignore Debra's questioning. "You have gym last period, right? I'll meet you at the side door."

"Okay," Debra said. She eyed Sharon knowingly. "And maybe *then* you'll tell me what's really got you in a daze." She breezed on, and Sharon looked after her, fondly.

Debra knew her so well. And Sharon wouldn't mind at all, confessing to Debra what had her so dazed. Dear Debra, who hadn't dated much, who had never even had a boyfriend—she was the one person Sharon could count on not to flaunt her sex life in her face.

Ten

Kris had been waiting for a summons to Mr. Quimby's office for two days. Ever since passing along her information about Paula Skinner to him on Monday morning, she'd been anticipating some big news. After all, even as she'd sat with him, he'd told the secretary to send Paula to his office. But then he'd asked Kris to leave before Paula arrived.

It was now Tuesday afternoon, last period, and she'd heard nothing about Paula's status as a homecoming queen candidate. Or about her own.

She twisted around in her seat and looked at Tracy Egan, three rows behind her. Maybe Tracy knows something, she thought. But she'd have to inquire very carefully. She didn't want the word getting around that she'd played any part in reporting Paula. Nor did she want people to know she had any expectations for herself.

Not that she was ashamed of what she'd done. Maybe it would hurt Paula, but it was for the

141

good of the school and its reputation. Even if Kris wasn't asked to replace Paula, she was glad Paula wouldn't have a chance to represent Greenwood. Kris had worked so hard to make herself respectable. She couldn't *bear* the thought of being associated with a school that would allow a—a *tramp* to become homecoming queen.

Still, the image of herself on the football field at half-time remained fixed in her head. She *had* to know what was going on! When the bell rang, she left the room, but she lingered just outside the door. When Tracy emerged, Kris maneuvered herself to walk by her side.

"Tracy, I just wanted to tell you that I'll let you know what time we'll be taping the show next week."

"Okay," Tracy replied.

"I haven't decided in what order I'll interview the candidates. Maybe you first, then Dana, then Veronica, and then Paula."

"Not Paula," Tracy murmured.

"What?"

"You won't be interviewing Paula," Tracy said sadly. "She's not a candidate anymore."

She's a good actress, Kris thought. She tried to equal Tracy's performance with her own reaction. "You're kidding! Paula dropped out?"

"She didn't drop out." There was just a hint of grimness in Tracy's voice. "Quimby took her out of the running."

"Why?"

Tracy didn't answer right away. After a moment, all she said was, "Better ask her."

142

Kris hid her exasperation. This was silly. The entire student body would know about Paula's condition soon, and here Tracy was pretending it was all hush-hush.

There was still another item of information Kris needed to get from Tracy, but she had to be very, very careful now. "Then I'll only have three candidates to interview?"

"No, there'll probably be four. Carl told me he got a note from Quimby telling him to have the football team pick another candidate."

Kris's heart leapt. "Did Carl happen to mention who the new candidate will be?" Afraid she might have sounded over-anxious, she hastily added, "I just need to know so I can get in touch with her about the interview."

"No," Tracy said. "I guess it will be announced some time this week."

By the time they parted, Kris's hands were clammy and it was all she could do to keep the elation out of her voice when she said good-bye. But she couldn't allow herself to get too excited. She didn't know for sure that the football team would select the nominee who'd had the next highest number of votes.

Still, as she breezed into the old chemistry lab for the meeting, she couldn't erase her happy smile. She greeted the others, even Jade, with an especially cheery hello. *Especially* Jade. After all, she owed the weirdo a debt of gratitude. If it hadn't been for Jade's good work, Kris might not have found out about Paula until it was too late.

But Jade didn't seem to appreciate Kris's

warm, heartfelt greeting. She didn't even respond. And if possible, she looked even sulkier than usual.

Jeff Russell was sitting on a table. "You guys are not going to recognize this room next week." He held up a large sheet of paper with blue sketching. "The people from Channel 42 are coming in this weekend to set up the place, turn it into a real television studio. This is how it's going to look." He pointed to different spots on the paper and started describing camera positions, lighting, and the stage.

As he went on, Kris began to daydream. Her imagination concocted the scene easily. She would interview each of the three candidates, and then, with just the right touch of humility, announce that she, too, was a candidate. Maybe Sharon could interview her. Or she could interview herself! That would be cute, and memorable, too. She'd stand out, maybe so much so that people would think only of her when they cast their votes the next day. Suddenly, visions of a crown began to float through her head.

But she was getting carried away. She shook off her fantasies and focused on Jeff.

"Tyler will open the show with a brief description of what it's all about. Then he'll introduce Sharon. Sharon, by the way, have you had any responses to your survey?"

"Not yet," Sharon replied. "But I've been talking to a lot of kids, so I've got a pretty good idea of what kind of answers I'll be getting."

"Can you give us a hint?" Tyler asked.

Sharon spoke so softly Kris had to strain to hear her. "Kids *are* having sex. Some use condoms, some don't."

"Do they realize how dangerous it is not to use protection?" Debra asked.

Sharon was almost inaudible. "I don't think they take it very seriously."

"Take what very seriously?" Jeff asked. "Using condoms or having sex?"

"Both."

Zack broke in. "I saw that survey of yours. Don't expect to get many back."

"What makes you say that?" Jeff asked.

"It's a joke. Everybody's laughing over it." He punctuated his remark with a cruel smile, directed at Sharon.

"That's not true," Tyler said. "*I've* seen people filling it out, and none of them were laughing."

Zack continued as if Tyler hadn't spoken. "Besides, it's too personal. I don't think Sharon should talk about this survey on television."

"Why not?" Debra asked. "I think it could be very interesting."

"It'll make Greenwood look bad," Zack declared. "We'll end up with a reputation that I, for one, don't want." He frowned. "There are some subjects that just shouldn't be talked about in public."

Jeff was watching him carefully. Then he said, "Good, good."

"Do you agree with him?" Sharon asked in alarm.

"I'm not taking sides. But this is exactly the

kind of argument and dialogue this show is supposed to present."

Zack wasn't pleased with this response at all. "We're going to come off looking like a bunch of fools. My father says—"

"Excuse me, Zack," Jeff interrupted. "With all due respect, your father isn't a member of this group. Kris, do you have anything to report?"

"I've got my questions for the homecoming queen candidates all planned," Kris told the group. "I'm going to ask about hobbies and school activities, and what being homecoming queen means to them. Then I'll ask about what they're planning to wear . . ."

"Fine, fine," Jeff said. "Be sure to tell the four candidates we'll be taping at two o'clock."

"I will," Kris replied, "but right now, there are only three. Paula Skinner isn't a candidate anymore."

For the first time at that meeting, Jade spoke. "Why?"

Kris's forehead puckered. Jade had to know perfectly well why Paula had been kicked off the ballot. She was just playing little Miss Innocent.

But now all the group members were looking at Kris, and expecting an answer. Unlike Tracy, Kris saw no reason to be evasive. Everyone would know soon enough. "She's pregnant."

There was a moment of silence. Sharon looked shocked, Tyler seemed embarrassed, and Zack shook his head in disgust. "And I always thought she was a *nice* girl," he muttered.

"I don't get it," Debra said.

146

"You don't get *what?*" Kris asked.

"Why she can't be a candidate. It's not like she'll be kicked out of school. Is there some sort of rule that says a homecoming queen can't be pregnant?"

"*Honestly,* Debra," Kris said. "Think how it would look."

Jade let out a harsh laugh. "Hypocrites."

"What's that supposed to mean?" Zack demanded to know.

Jade nodded toward Sharon. "First, she says everyone at this school is having sex. Then this girl Paula gets pregnant and you all act horrified. So what's the deal here? It's okay to have sex, but don't let it show?" She looked around the group, as if daring them to answer her.

Debra took up the challenge. "I think Jade's making a good point. It's kind of a double standard, isn't it?"

"It doesn't matter," Kris said. "She's out."

"Then you won't need as much time for your interview segment, will you," Jeff commented.

"Oh, there's going to be a fourth candidate," Kris assured him.

"Who is it?" Tyler asked.

Kris ducked her head, just in case her expression might betray her. "I don't know yet."

As the meeting broke up, Sharon was still trying to absorb Kris's news. Paula Skinner was pregnant.

Of course, she wasn't the first girl at Green-

147

wood High to get pregnant. But she was the first girl Sharon knew personally.

Paula lived just two houses away from her. Their mothers were good friends. As children, Sharon and Paula had played together, took swimming lessons at the Y together, attended each other's birthday parties.

After elementary school, however, they didn't see much of each other socially. The one-year gap in their ages became important once they hit middle school age. But when Sharon ran into Paula, at school or in the neighborhood, she was always friendly. And once in a while they shared a laugh over some remembered childhood escapade. Sharon had been pleased when she'd heard Paula was a homecoming queen candidate.

And now she was pregnant. Sharon was having a hard time dealing with this. Like that jerk Zack said, Paula *was* a nice girl.

But then, so were most of those other girls who were having sex. Paula—and her boyfriend—had just been careless.

She was thinking about this as she left the meeting with Debra. Debra was still fuming about Zack's comments. "I don't trust that guy. We'd better keep an eye on him. I can see him trying to sabotage the show, just so he can come off as the model citizen."

"Mm."

"What's the matter?" Debra asked.

"I was thinking about Paula."

"Oh, that's right, you know her. I can't *believe* Quimby made her quit the race." Then she sighed. "What am I saying? Of *course* I can believe it. It's a typical Quimby move. Wait'll Quimby sees this television show. He's going to freak."

Sharon had to smile. "For someone who was never interested in school activities, you sound like you're enjoying this."

"I am," Debra admitted. "I really enjoyed doing the research and digging up those facts. When I do that for a school paper, I always feel a little let down afterwards, knowing that the only person to see the work will be my teacher. But this is going on television! It'll be fun, listening to you report what we've discovered."

"Maybe for the next show, *you'll* actually appear on the air yourself."

Debra made a face. "I don't want *that* much fun."

Sharon wanted to stop in the restroom, so they parted. Inside, Jade was leaning against a wall, smoking a cigarette.

"Better watch out," Sharon advised her. "Gym teachers check in here all the time." She expected Jade to sneer at this, but Jade actually stuck the cigarette under running water and then tossed it into a wastebasket.

This encouraged Sharon to continue a conversation. "I liked what you said in the meeting, Jade. About the double standard."

Jade shrugged. Sharon took a brush out of her handbag and gave her hair a few half-hearted swipes.

"Was it like this at your old school?"

"Yeah, I guess so. There are hypocrites everywhere."

"It must have been hard for you, leaving your school."

"Yeah."

On an impulse, Sharon asked, "Did you have a boyfriend there? I don't mean to be nosy, I'm just the curious type."

"Yeah."

"Are you still seeing him?"

"No, we broke up before I transferred."

"Oh." Sharon didn't dare ask why. That would *really* be nosy. But Jade actually supplied more information on her own.

"He wanted to do things I wasn't into."

Sharon faced her directly. "You mean, like . . . sex?"

"No." Jade smiled slightly. "If I hadn't had sex with him, he'd have been long gone a lot earlier. Like most guys."

"Oh. Right."

"He was into drugs," Jade said bluntly. "Does that shock you?"

"No. But I'm glad you're not into them."

"You don't have a big drug problem here at Greenwood, do you?"

"I don't think so."

"But you *do* have sex."

Sharon turned back to the mirror. "Not everyone does."

"Yeah? You want some advice?"

"Sure."

"Don't hold out too long. Not if you want to

150

hang on to him. For once, Jade's voice didn't drip with sarcasm. She sounded almost nice. And a little . . . sad.

"Is that the reason we're supposed to have sex?" Sharon said quietly. "To hold on to a guy, keep him from dumping us? What about love?"

"Sex is the way to show love," Jade replied. "I guess. Just don't get pregnant."

That made Sharon think of Paula again. "I wonder how Quimby found out about Paula. It's not like she's showing yet."

She was startled to see a cloud come over Jade's face. "I have to go," she said bluntly. And she left the restroom.

She's a strange girl, Sharon thought. But interesting. And now she had another opinion on the subject that occupied her mind. Another point of view, to add to all the others. But all the opinions, all the points of view, they added up to one thing.

They were all pointing her in the same direction. To say, yes.

Eleven

Sharon rarely slept late, even on weekends. But on Saturday morning, she couldn't seem to drag herself out of bed. Lying there, she drifted from half-awake to restless sleep, consciously unwilling to face the reality of the day. During one of those half-awake times, she thought it might not be a bad idea to spend the whole day this way.

A ringing phone forced her to abandon her plans. It rang four times before she accepted the fact that no one else was home, and she reached for the extension by her bed.

"Hello?"

"Hi, it's me."

Sharon propped herself up on an elbow and tried to sound reasonably alert. "Hi, Deb. What's up?"

"Not much. Did you hear the announcement last period yesterday?"

"Yeah. Pretty wild, huh? Kris must be ecstatic."

"But what about her segment on the show?" Debra asked. "Is she going to interview *herself*?"

"I haven't the slightest idea," Sharon replied. The last thing she wanted to concern herself with was Kris's interview. But she couldn't resist teasing Debra. "Maybe Jeff will ask *you* to do it."

"I don't mind if he asks."

"Really?"

"As long as he doesn't mind when I say no. Hey, did you get any of your surveys back?"

"No, none."

"Well, you've still got a few days before the show," Debra said. "Maybe they'll come in."

Sharon envisioned herself reading page after page about her classmates' sexual exploits. She sank back on her pillow. "Yeah, maybe."

"You don't sound too thrilled about the prospect."

She wasn't. "I'm just wiped out today, I guess."

"Are you going out with Tyler tonight?"

"Yes. Listen, I've got to go. My mother's calling me. Talk to you later, okay?"

Listlessly, she hung up the phone. Had she ever lied to Debra before in order to get off the phone? Probably not. But as she lay there, she did hear some noises coming from downstairs. She dragged herself out of bed and pulled on a robe.

Kyle was sprawled on the living-room floor, playing with a Gameboy. MTV blasted out of the television. The volume told her there were no parents in the house.

"Where are the folks?" she asked him.

"Grocery shopping," Kyle replied.

She gazed at the TV screen for a moment.

153

While the words of the song were unintelligible, the images told a clear story. A young, beautiful woman in lingerie that allowed her to show lots of cleavage, cavorted on a bed with a good-looking guy. Nothing really happened, but a lot was suggested. There was a close-up of the guy's face, smiling, his eyes closed. Then there was a close-up of the woman, her lips parted, her head arched backward. It was pretty obvious what was going on.

Kyle was working his game, but he glanced every now and then at the TV. He showed no reaction to what was happening on the screen. Watching music videos as much as he did, he must see stuff like this all the time, Sharon thought. It wouldn't shock him.

And why should it? It was only sex. No big deal.

Hearing the back door open, she went into the kitchen. "Here, give me that," she said to her mother, relieving her of one of the bags she was juggling.

"Thanks, honey." And then she yelled, "Kyle, turn that down right this minute."

Her father plunked his bags on the kitchen table. "I guess I should start putting this stuff away," he said, but his anxious eyes were on the clock.

Mrs. Delaney gave him an amused look. "What time does the game start?"

"You go watch, Dad," Sharon said. "I'll help in here."

He made his escape. Sharon began pulling

food out of the bags. Looking up, she caught her mother's quizzical observation of her appearance.

"I just got up," Sharon explained.

"Do you feel all right?"

For some reason, the question annoyed her. "I'm fine," she replied testily. "Can't a person sleep late once in a while without having to stand trial?" She immediately regretted her tone. "Sorry. I've got a lot on my mind. The TV show, you know."

"Have you chosen a title for it yet?"

"No." She opened a cabinet and began putting canned goods inside. Even with her back turned, she sensed her mother's eyes on her. And when she turned to face her, those eyes shifted too quickly.

"Are *you* all right?" she asked her mother.

"Fine, dear, just fine."

"Something's bugging you."

Mrs. Delaney hesitated a fraction of a second. "I . . . wasn't going to say anything. You know that I believe teenagers deserve space, and I try never to pry into your personal life—"

"Spill it, Mom!"

Her mother sighed. "Well, I did a load of laundry last Friday night, and I went into your room to leave your clothes. The screen to your computer was on, and I couldn't help looking. There were these questions . . ." Her voice trailed off.

"It was a survey," Sharon said. "For the TV show."

Relief flooded her mother's face. "Oh, I see."

Sharon waited, dreading—or maybe hoping—for more questions. But her mother changed the subject.

"The supermarket was packed today. I ran into Audrey Skinner there."

"Did she tell you Paula isn't a homecoming queen candidate anymore?"

"Yes."

"Did she say why?" When her mother hesitated, Sharon said, "It's okay, I know she's pregnant. I'm sure practically everyone at school does by now."

Mrs. Delaney nodded. "It's sad. But Audrey says they're all handling it pretty well. And it's not like it was in my day, when something like this ruined a girl's life."

"Were you shocked? I mean, you've known Paula since she was little."

Her mother shook her head ruefully. "I know kids . . . mature earlier these days. I try to be open-minded. Still, it's too bad. Especially since this could have been avoided. Sharon . . ."

"Don't worry, Mom. I'm not going to get pregnant." She held up a pack of chicken parts. "Freezer?"

"Please."

She popped them in. That was the last item in the bag. "I'm going to get dressed."

Back up in her room, she pulled on jeans and a t-shirt, and made her bed. She'd planned to spend the morning writing up her report for the TV show. But it wasn't something she wanted to think about.

She went to her closet, with the idea of selecting what she'd wear for her date with Tyler. But she didn't want to think about that either.

She didn't want to think. Period. She went downstairs and secured permission to take the car to the mall.

Driving was good for her. The need to watch and concentrate kept everything else out of her mind. Hopefully, the attractions of the mall would continue to distract her.

The first distraction she wanted was food. She hadn't bothered with breakfast, and it was now lunch time. At the huge, three-level shopping center, she had a variety of options from which to choose. She passed the Chirping Chicken and the Taco Fiesta, scanning the seating areas to see if by chance anyone she knew was around.

She hated eating alone in public. She always imagined people passing her and thinking, *poor girl, she has no friends*. She paused at La Creperie, and her eyes lit on a sole figure, just sitting down at a table. A coincidence, when she'd just been talking about her that morning.

"Hi, Paula."

"Sharon, hi! Are you going to eat? Get your food and join me." She indicated her plate. "Try the spinach and cheese ones, they're terrific."

A moment later, Sharon returned with a spinach and cheese crepe. Paula was just starting on her second. "It's funny, last week the very thought of food made me nauseous. Now I can't eat enough."

"Are you feeling okay now?"

"Mm. Thanks for sitting with me. There are a lot of kids who wouldn't, now." She paused. "You know what I'm talking about, don't you?"

Sharon nodded.

"I guess everyone will pretty soon," Paula said matter-of-factly. "Well, I wouldn't be able to keep it a secret for long, would I?"

"You're going to have the baby?"

"Yes, and I'm going to keep it. And I can guess what your next question is going to be. No, Billy and I are not getting married. Not right away, at least."

"What about school?"

"I'll stay, and graduate. Unless the baby comes early. Then I'll finish up in summer school."

"You're so calm about it," Sharon blurted out.

Paula fell silent. She concentrated on scraping the last of the crepe off her plate. "I wasn't, at first," she finally said. "I was a basket case. But I'm lucky, I guess. Billy's sticking by me, my family's supportive . . . . I can still go to Georgia State here in town this fall, and my folks said we can hire someone to help out with the baby."

Sharon was in awe. "I think it's great, the way you're dealing with it."

Paula gave her a slight smile. "You're not shocked? You don't think I'm a slut?"

"Good grief, no!" She noticed Paula gazing longingly at her unfinished crepe. She moved the plate toward her. "Here, you want the rest of this? I'm not' hungry."

"Thanks." Paula took a bit and chewed pensively. "A lot of kids *are* shocked. I can tell who knows about it, from the way they look at me in the halls at school." She pushed the plate away. "Oh, let's not talk about it anymore."

Sharon noticed the shopping bag at Paula's feet. "What did you buy?"

"Actually, it's something I'm about to return. The gown I bought to wear for homecoming. I won't be needing it."

"I think that stinks," Sharon said vehemently. "Why shouldn't you still be a homecoming queen candidate?"

Paula gave a short laugh. "According to Mr. Quimby, it sets a bad example for other students."

"That's insane," Sharon sputtered. "Like, he thinks they're all so innocent? It doesn't make any sense at all."

"I know. But what can I do?"

"You don't have to give in to him." She leaned forward. "Paula, did you want to be homecoming queen?"

"It wasn't the most important thing in the world to me," Paula replied. Then she smiled, a little sadly. "But it would have been a hoot, I guess."

"Then don't let a jerk like Quimby get you down," Sharon stated. "Show the kids you haven't done anything to be ashamed of. Okay, you made a mistake, not taking precautions. Or maybe, it was an accident. But so what? Maybe they could learn something." She stopped suddenly. "Geez, I sound like I'm giving you a lecture."

Paula gazed at her warmly. "That's okay. You

159

always were a fighter. Well, if you come up with any brilliant notions on how to get me back on the ballot, let me know." She looked at her watch. "I have to get home."

"Paula," Sharon said as the older girl rose from the table.

"What?"

"Don't return the dress. Not just yet."

Why had she said that, Sharon wondered after leaving her. Was she going to turn Paula's situation into one of her 'causes?' Or was she just looking for a way not to think about her own problems?

She looked into store windows through unseeing eyes. Window shopping, without the money or the need for anything major, had never much appealed to her. She racked her brain for a mission, an errand, something small and cheap she could buy so the time wouldn't be a total waste.

A display in a pharmacy window caught her eye. It was for a new hair conditioner, guaranteed to provide shine and body and a close resemblance to some glamorous movie star. Fingering her limp hair, Sharon doubted the claims of the product, but it was on sale and she'd at least have something to show for her trip to the mall.

She went inside, located the conditioner, and took the bottle to the cashier at the counter. It was there that she saw another display.

Condoms. Little boxes of them, hanging from a rack, easy to pick up and add to your purchases. You didn't even have to ask for them.

She must have passed displays like this a million times without even a glance. This time, she stared at the rack, hypnotized, unable to tear her eyes away. What she had been blocking, avoiding, refusing to think about, came rushing back into her mind like a tidal wave. Tonight. Tyler. What would he expect from her? What would she need to do, if she wanted to hold on to him?

But Tyler would be prepared, she told herself. Then she recalled what one of the girls had said at lunch the other day. A girl had to watch out for herself. This was her responsibility, as much as his.

Furtively, she studied the display. Thank goodness, no one else was at the counter. There were so many different kinds. Colors, even.

"Can I help you?" the girl behind the counter asked impatiently.

Sharon moved fast, and snatched the pack closest to her. The girl didn't bat an eye as she rang up the conditioner and the condoms. She popped them both in a bag and handed it over.

It was a brown bag, and no one could see through it, but Sharon stuffed it in her handbag anyway. It would be just her luck to run into someone she knew who would ask her what she'd just bought.

She almost smiled at her concern. Given the attitude of the other kids at school, she could wear the box around her neck and no one would even blink.

* * *

She dressed slowly that evening, picking each item with care. A silky camisole. A sarong skirt, with a softly flowered shirt. Small gold earrings. Pantyhose? No, they could be awkward.

It seemed to her that she was moving like a robot, stiffly, automatically. She felt as if her mind was detached from her body, like she was planning something that was about to happen to someone else.

She put on makeup she rarely wore—eye shadow and mascara. She outlined her lips before applying lipstick. She applied gel to her hair and sprayed cologne liberally. Then she stepped away from the mirror to examine herself, objectively. She could really do that too, be objective, because she felt like she was looking at someone else.

I look good, she thought. Better than good.

She wondered if she'd look the same tomorrow. Did it change a girl? She'd read that somewhere, in a romance novel, that a girl was different after making love for the very first time.

"Sharon! Tyler's here."

At the sound of her mother's voice, she tensed. Then, taking a deep breath, she went downstairs.

"Hi, how are you." To her ears, her own voice seemed to be coming from far away.

Tyler didn't notice. His eyes widened as he took in her appearance. "You look fantastic."

"So do you," she replied automatically, and they both smiled at their joke. She relaxed a little.

"Where are you two going?" her father asked.

"The movies," Tyler told him.

Sharon noticed for the first time that her father

was wearing a suit, and her mother was in her best black cocktail dress. "Are you going out?" she asked.

"Big dinner dance," her father said.

"And Kyle's spending the night at a friend's," her mother added. "Do you have your keys? We won't be back till very late."

Sharon nodded. They all said their good-byes and wished each other a good time.

On the way to the movie theater, they talked about school, the TV program, the upcoming homecoming game. "There's no way Greenwood can win," Tyler said. "Winding Creek was number two in the state last year."

"I know."

"Well, I guess we can cheer ourselves up at the dance afterward."

"Mm."

He stopped at a red light. "Can we?"

She hadn't really been listening. "Can we what?"

"Cheer ourselves up at the dance. You and me."

"All right," she said. Then, aware of how dull she must sound, she pulled herself together and attempted a dazzling smile. "I'd love to."

"Great." And then he groaned. "Oh no, look at that line."

Sharon looked. The line in front of the movie theater stretched out endlessly.

"And it's just started to rain," she noted.

"Do you really want to see this movie?" Tyler asked.

"Not particularly."

"Then how about this. Why don't we pick up a couple of videos and go back to your place?"

"Okay," Sharon said faintly. Curious, she thought as they drove on, how no one but yourself can hear your heart beat, even when it sounds like a hundred pounding drums.

"And I . . . uh, I brought my guitar."

Turning, Sharon saw the case on the back seat, and she was pleased. Not only because Tyler was going to share his music with her. But also because guitar playing required two hands.

At the video store, they selected one comedy and one drama. They stopped at a convenience store, to pick up chips and popcorn and sodas. Then they drove back to Sharon's house.

The house was dark. As soon as they entered, Sharon hurried around the living-room, turning on lights. She busied herself sticking the popcorn in the microwave, putting chips in a bowl, pouring sodas.

Tyler was working the VCR. "Which one do you want to watch first?"

"The funny one," Sharon said promptly. She figured it was least likely to create a certain mood. They sat on the sofa, side by side, and Sharon operated the remote control.

For a while, they watched the film and nibbled on the munchies she'd laid out on the coffee table. The movie was some silly, slapstick business, and it wasn't really very funny. At least, Sharon didn't think so. But maybe that was because her thoughts were elsewhere.

At that very moment, her thoughts were on her shoulders, around which Tyler had draped his arm. Again, as in other times, it felt nice, comfortable. She had a sudden urge to snuggle closer, to place her head on his chest. A slight tightening of his hand on her shoulder made her suspect he wouldn't mind if she did just that.

He leaned over and kissed her, a long, gentle kiss. That was nice too, but she couldn't really enjoy it. Her mind was racing, trying to visualize what would happen next, so that she could be prepared.

But after the kiss, Tyler spoke. "Your parents seem nice."

Surprised by the topic, all Sharon could say was, "Yeah."

"Can you talk to them?" Tyler asked. "Really talk to them, about personal stuff?"

She thought about that. "We get along pretty well, but . . . no, not really."

"It's the same for me," Tyler said. "They're super people, but everytime I try to bring up something like my music, they seem to turn off. They're just not *there*."

Sharon thought about her unsatisfactory conversation that morning with her mother. "I know what you mean."

"Do you ever feel sometimes like you're talking to them, and they're listening, but they're not actually hearing you?"

"Yes!" Sharon exclaimed. "You feel like you're speaking a foreign language that they don't understand."

"And there's no connection," Tyler said.

"Exactly. It's as if something's missing." She pointed at the TV. "Like, if you pulled out one of those wires connecting the cable box to the TV, and you got the picture but no sound—"

"That's just what I was thinking!" Tyler said.

There was a moment of silent appreciation between them. "With you," Tyler said slowly, "I feel connected."

"Me, too," Sharon whispered.

"I've never known a girl I could talk to like this. I feel like we can tell each other anything."

There was a question in his eyes as he spoke, and she answered, "Yes." She did feel very close to him. "Do you want to watch any more of this movie?"

"Not particularly."

"It's pretty awful," she agreed. "Should I put the other one on?"

"Do you want to see it?"

"Not really." She hit the stop button, and then the off button. "I'd rather hear your music."

He was pleased, she could tell. He took the guitar out of the case, and strummed a few experimental chords. Then his fingers began working the strings expertly, and what emerged was a pulsating, rhythmic tune that filled the air. Sharon's body began to move involuntarily to the strong, driving beat.

When he stopped, she applauded. "That was fantastic! Tyler, you're really talented!"

He reddened slightly. "That wasn't anything special, just something I whipped up ages ago."

"Okay, then play me something special," Sharon demanded.

"Well, there's something I wrote last week. It's not really finished . . ." He gazed at her through anxious eyes. She nodded encouragingly.

He started playing a melody, a strange, haunting, beautiful tune. After a moment he began to sing.

"In your eyes I see, my fears and hopes and dreams, and yet it seems, I can't see you. In your eyes I see, what you want me to know, but even so, I can't see you . . ."

Could a voice be rough and soothing at the same time? There was no one word to describe it, Sharon thought. In his words, she heard yearning and sadness and a million other emotions.

"Take off the mask, and let me see, please open your eyes to me."

His voice faded away, and the last chord hung in the air. He put the guitar down and looked at her.

Sharon was speechless. She'd suspected he'd be a good musician, but she had no idea he was *this* good.

And this moving. She felt like she'd just been told something incredibly personal and intimate, and she was in awe. Never, never before had she felt so linked, so tied to another human being. "Tyler . . . that was . . ." she struggled for a

167

word. Beautiful, wonderful, fabulous—they were all inadequate words. "Magical," she finally whispered.

But there was no real need for words. He took her in his arms, and her mind went blank as she allowed the feelings to take over.

She wanted him, closer and closer. She wanted them to belong to each other, to become inseparable, to communicate in a way she'd never communicated with anyone before.

He read her mind. "Do you want to . . ."

"Yes . . ."

Then there began new feelings, new sensations, unfamiliar, thrilling ones. For a while, she allowed herself to enjoy them, to take joy in the unfamiliar, exciting experience . . .

And then, suddenly, like the flick of a light switch in a pitch-black room, panic hit her with a flash. "No," she said. And then, louder, "No!"

He pulled away, but he kept an arm around her. "What's the matter?"

"Just . . . just don't." She pushed his arm off her. "Don't touch me."

"Sharon!" Confusion was written all over his face. "Please tell me what's going on!"

It's not right, not yet, she wanted to scream. I can't go this far, I'm not ready for this. We have to wait, the time isn't right, not yet. Not for me.

But she couldn't admit this. It was so much easier just to shake her head.

"Tell me what you're thinking," he pleaded. "Talk to me. I don't understand."

"What difference would it make?" she cried

out. Because he *wouldn't* understand, he could *never* understand. He wouldn't want to wait, and why should he? No other girl would demand this of him. She was weird, a freak, an oddity, incapable of loving to the fullest.

He stared at her in utter disbelief. "What do you want me to do?"

"I want you to leave."

There was no more confusion, no more disbelief. He stood up. When he spoke, his voice was cold. "What about homecoming?"

She couldn't speak. All she knew was that she couldn't bear going through another experience like this. She shook her head, no. Then she turned, so she wouldn't have to see his reaction. But she heard the door slam when he left.

He was gone. She'd lost him, just like the other girls said she would. And all that was left for her to do now was cry, helplessly. Hopelessly.

Twelve

As Jeff promised, the old chemistry lab had been completely transformed. By the time Kris arrived for the program run-through on Wednesday, everything was in place.

The big room was spotlessly clean and freshly painted. Big lights were suspended from the ceiling. Stepping over the wires on the floor, Kris examined the rising rows of bleachers where the audience would sit. She passed two cameras mounted on pedestals. They were pointed in the general direction of a small stage on which an arrangement of chairs had been placed. It wasn't a chemistry lab anymore. It was a real television studio.

Kris took a seat on the stage, and imagined doing the adorable self-interview she'd prepared. The show would be aired tomorrow night at five o'clock. By six o'clock, she'd be the most talked about girl at Greenwood High. And on Friday, when the students voted for homecoming queen, she just might make Greenwood history as the first queen from the junior class.

She'd brushed off that fantasy a few days ago. Now, she allowed herself to pursue it. Oh, the difference just becoming a candidate had made in her life! She recalled her fears of just a few weeks ago, when she'd been forced to give up cheerleading after her accident. She'd been so afraid she'd become a nobody!

She wasn't afraid anymore. Kids she barely knew, seniors even, had rushed to congratulate her on her candidacy. A junior member of the football team, Mike Carey, had asked her out for Saturday night. He wasn't exactly the man of her dreams, but she'd gone out with him, and during the evening she'd secured his services as escort for homecoming. She was getting more attention than she'd ever received in her life. Now, she was going to be on television, in the limelight, which would secure this attention well beyond homecoming.

And she'd done it all by herself. Well, with a little help from Jade. She'd have to remember to thank her. Privately, with nobody looking, of course.

There was the sound of approaching footsteps. A moment later, Jade ambled into the studio. It was perfect timing, Kris thought. She had to move quickly, now, before the others arrived.

She switched on her brightest smile. "Jade, how are you?"

She wasn't expecting much in the way of a

friendly greeting from Jade. But she wasn't prepared for the girl to radiate such intense dislike.

"You used me," Jade said bluntly.

"What are you talking about?"

"That's why you wanted me to get the dirt on those girls. So you could get one of them kicked off the ballot and become a candidate for queen yourself."

Kris was momentarily taken aback. Then she pretended to be hurt by the accusation, and denied it. "Jade, how can you say that? I had nothing to do with Paula getting taken off the ballot."

Jade's response was succinct. "Bull." She strode away and sat down on the edge of a bleacher.

Alarmed, Kris followed her. What did Jade know? The last thing she needed was for Jade to start telling people that she, Kris, had told Mr. Quimby about Paula's pregnancy. Rapidly, she considered her options. What could she do to keep Jade from talking? Offer a bribe? A threat? Something told her nothing would have an impact on her.

Except maybe shifting the guilt. She dropped all pretense of innocence, sat down on the bleacher beside Jade, and faced her squarely. "Actually, when you think about it, this whole business is your fault, Jade."

Jade's eyes narrowed. "Huh?"

Kris leaned in closer. "You didn't *have* to ask around about Paula, or any of the girls for that matter. Nobody held a gun to your head. You didn't have to tell me what you learned." She

172

rose and gazed down at Jade triumphantly. "You're the one responsible for what happened to Paula. Not me."

She only had time to enjoy a brief glimpse of Jade's stricken expression. The others were coming in, and she had to distance herself.

Zack approached her, looking a lot more friendly than he ever had before. "Congratulations, Kris."

Kris ducked her head demurely. "Thank you, Zack. I can't tell you what a surprise it was to me."

"I wasn't surprised."

Kris's smile became stiff. Had Jade already said something? "You weren't?"

"Hell, no. I was surprised when you weren't nominated in the first go-round."

It took Kris a few seconds before his attitude and tone registered. Then it hit her. He was flirting! Zack Stevenson, major Greenwood big shot, the rich son of a state senator, a guy who'd never given her a second look was now coming on to her!

"Zack, could I see you?" Jeff called.

It was with obvious reluctance that he left her. Kris could have kicked herself. If only she'd waited before asking what's-his-name, Mike, the second string football player, to escort her to homecoming. Maybe she could break the date and invite Zack, instead. No, the word would get around school. She tried to be philosophical. At least she knew Zack was interested—and once again, she marveled at the success of her scheme.

173

She'd expected the other kids to surround her with their congratulations, but none appeared to be forthcoming. Debra and Sharon were huddled together on the second tier of the bleachers. Tyler was sitting on the edge of the stage. And now Jeff Russell was calling for everyone's attention.

"Before we begin our run-through, we need to make a change in our plans." He looked a little harried as he ran his fingers through his hair. "Kris, I understand you're now a candidate for homecoming queen. That creates a problem with your interview segment."

Kris shook her head. "I've thought about that, and I've got a solution. After I interview the other girls, I'll interview myself! It'll be different, and I think the audience would get a real kick out of that."

She looked around at the others for support. Zack gave her a nod of approval. But it was immediately apparent that everyone else thought she was nuts.

Including Jeff. "Kris, it won't work. Since you're a candidate, there's a serious conflict of interest here. Someone else will have to conduct the interviews."

Kris pouted. "But Jeff, I'm all prepared!"

"I'm sorry, Kris. And I'm not suggesting that you might take advantage of your position as interviewer. But it could look that way to the audience, and we can't risk it."

Zack spoke up. "I thought you said *we* were running this show."

Jeff eyed him thoughtfully. "You're right, Zack.

Let's put this to a vote. All those in favor of Kris interviewing the candidates and herself?" Only Kris and Zack raised their hands. "Opposed? Tyler, are you abstaining?"

"Oh. Sorry." Tyler lifted a hand briefly.

Inwardly, Kris was seething, but she fought back her annoyance and smiled bravely. "That's all right. There will be other shows. But who's going to do the interviews?"

Jeff gazed around the room. "Debra, how about you?"

"No, thanks," Debra said promptly. "I don't mean to sound like a bad sport, but I only agreed to work on this program if I could stay off camera."

Jeff started to argue. "But Debra—"

A rarely heard voice interrupted. "I'll do it."

All the faces that turned in the direction of Jade bore the same disbelief.

"You want to interview the homecoming queens?" Jeff asked.

"Yes," she stated, with an expression that dared any of them to argue the matter.

"Well, fine," Jeff said uncertainly. "Kris, you can give your notes to Jade. Let's get on with our run-through."

Kris was aware of a cold chill creeping up her spine. "Uh, Jeff, could I have a few minutes alone with Jade first? So I can fill her in on the stuff that's not in the notes."

Jeff checked his watch. "We're pretty pressed for time, Kris. Five minutes, okay?"

Kris beckoned to Jade, who followed her to an

area behind the bleachers. Once Kris was certain that no one else could see her or hear her, she fixed fearful eyes on Jade.

"What do you think you're up to?"

"I don't know what you mean," Jade replied cooly.

"If you think for one minute you're going to make me look like a fool on TV—"

"You don't need me to make you look like a fool." Jade smirked. "I'll bet you can do that all by yourself."

Kris was frantic. She dropped all pretense, and let her anger show. "I'm warning you. If you say one word that I don't like in that interview, I swear, I'll make your life miserable."

The threat didn't faze Jade. "It already is."

Jeff's voice floated to the back of the room. "Come on, folks, we have to get going."

Kris turned away from Jade.

"Hey, wait a minute," Jade said.

With her back still turned, Kris allowed herself a brief smile of triumph. "What?"

"The notes." Jade held out her hand.

Kris practically threw them at her. As she went to rejoin the group, she tried to control the nausea that seemed to fill her. Could that wretched little hoodlum destroy her reputation?

No, she answered herself. It was impossible. Because it didn't really matter what Jade said, even on TV. Who would pay attention to a person who looked like *that*?

Still, she would have to keep her guard up during the interview, and be very, very careful. That

wouldn't be difficult for her. She'd had her **guard** up for years.

Tyler read from his notes. "Thank you for watching. We'll be back next week with another edition of . . ." He stopped and looked at Jeff, who threw his hands in the air.

"Say anything for now."

Tyler paused for a second, and then shrugged. "The Greenwood High Hour."

"Sounds dull," Debra murmured to Sharon.

"Then it fits the show," Sharon whispered back.

With a smile that was clearly taking effort, Jeff spoke with forced cheer. "Good job, folks. A few minor suggestions . . . . Tyler, try to put some expression in your voice. And maybe you could memorize your introductions, okay?"

"Okay," Tyler said, in the same flat tone he'd used throughout the run-through.

"And Jade . . . I realize you haven't had any time to prepare, but you really need to demonstrate some enthusiasm in your interview."

Only the slightest head movement indicated that Jade was listening to him.

"Sharon, I didn't hear much enthusiasm from you either."

"Sorry," Sharon said. "I guess I'm a little nervous. "*What a joke*, she thought sadly. Nervous wasn't the word at all. Throughout her presentation, with Tyler always in view, it was all she could do to keep her voice from cracking. Talking about sex, how everyone was having it, how it was no big deal, and knowing he was listening to every word she said . . . She'd felt like a fraud. And a freak.

"And Zack, don't pound on the table when you do your rebuttal, okay?"

"I was driving home a point," Zack argued.

"We got it," Jeff said. He surveyed the group. "Why are you all looking so down? I promise, with the audience in here tomorrow, it's going to come alive. Tyler, be sure to watch for hands going up."

"What if I don't see any hands?" Tyler asked.

"Then just stick the microphone in someone's face and say, 'what do you think about that?' "

Zack snorted. "What if he doesn't see any audience?"

In a completely different tone, Debra asked, "How *are* we going to get kids to come?"

Jeff grinned. "Why do you think I arranged to have the taping at two o'clock? Anyone coming to the show gets excused from last period."

"Brilliant!" Debra exclaimed.

Zack didn't appear to think so. "Does Mr. Quimby know about this? I don't think it's so brilliant to let students sacrifice an hour of education."

Sharon saw Tyler's lips move to form the words, 'pompous ass,' and then their eyes met. She had an urge to grin and nod in agreement. But she fought it back and looked away.

"Mr. Quimby knows, and he's agreed to let us tape during school hours this one time," Jeff

178

said. "Now, I've had tickets printed up, and I'm giving each of you twenty to distribute. Be here tomorrow, no later than 1:30."

"What should we wear?" Kris asked.

"What you normally wear," Jeff replied. "Don't get dressed up. Remember, this is a show about real young adults talking about real young adult problems. So you should look—real."

Debra spoke into Sharon's ear. "Can't you just picture Jade with the homecoming girls? What a hoot!"

"A riot," Sharon mumbled glumly.

"But we still don't have a real title," Jeff said. "And if we don't come up with one right now, we're going to have to call it—what was it you said, Tyler?"

"The Greenwood High Hour."

"What do the rest of you think of that?"

There was a general rumble of discontent. Jeff was beginning to look impatient. "Then give me something else. Sharon? Do you have any ideas?"

All eyes turned to her. Except for one pair. Tyler was contemplating the ceiling.

Sharon struggled for something, anything. "What does the administration call us?"

"The TV club," Jeff told her.

"TV club," Sharon repeated. "TV club. That sounds juvenile. How about the video club?"

"Club sounds too exclusive," Debra said. "This is supposed to be for all high school students."

"'Video High,'" Tyler said.

"Perfect!" Sharon exclaimed. Tyler started to

smile, and then he caught himself and looked away.

"Not bad at all," Jeff echoed. " 'Video High.' What do the rest of you think?"

This time the rumble was more upbeat.

"Then 'Video High' it is," Jeff stated. "That's it, folks. See you tomorrow."

Sharon didn't move right away. She watched as Tyler rose and stood there, scratching his head. Then he began searching through his back pack for something.

"Go talk to him," Debra urged.

"About what?" Sharon shook her head. "There's nothing to talk about."

Tyler finally left, and she rose. "Let's go."

"I have to stop at my locker," Debra said. "I'll meet you at yours."

There were only a few people wandering the halls that late in the afternoon. Turning the combination of her locker, Sharon saw Jade down the hall, closing hers.

A moment later, Jade walked by. "Hi," Sharon said.

Jade nodded, and paused. "Listen . . ."

"What?"

"Do you think Jeff meant it? About dressing like we always do?"

"Sure."

Jade made a vague gesture. "Like . . . this?"

"Why not?" Sharon slammed her locker shut. "You have your own personal look. It suits you."

Jade searched Sharon's face for signs of teasing. Apparently, she didn't find any. But her expression remained defiant. "I don't exactly fit Greenwood's image though, do I?"

Sharon was in no mood to tiptoe around Jade. "But that's what you want, isn't it?" she asked.

Jade stiffened, and Sharon immediately regretted her bluntness. She tried to make up for it. "It was nice of you to volunteer to take over Kris's job."

Jade immediately went on the defensive. "I'll bet you were shocked."

"Yes," Sharon admitted. "I didn't think you'd be all that interested in interviewing homecoming queen candidates."

"I'm not," Jade replied quickly. "You want to know why I volunteered?" Her expression issued a challenge.

Sharon sighed. "Sure. Why?"

"So I could make fun of them. So I could get them to show what jerks they all are. Right on TV."

Sharon wasn't surprised. This was pretty much what she expected from Jade. But the girl's attitude was beginning to get on her nerves. "Why do you want to do that, Jade? What's the point? What good will it do?"

"Because . . . because . . ." Jade floundered. "Because they're jerks. Homecoming queens. What a lame concept. I want everyone to see them for what they are."

"In *your* opinion," Sharon pointed out.

"Oh, I get it," Jade said wisely. "You wish you could be homecoming queen, too."

Sharon struggled to remain calm. "No, that

sort of thing doesn't appeal to me. All I'm saying is that they're not all jerks. Tracy Egan is nice. And Paula—but she's not a candidate anymore."

"Yeah, I know."

For a split second, Sharon thought she saw Jade's lower lip tremble. Then she pressed her lips together so tightly they practically turned white, and she spit out the next words. "I made that happen."

At first, Sharon thought Jade was still just trying to shock her. But there was something in Jade's face, an odd combination of hostility and shame, that caught her attention. "How did you do that?"

She listened to Jade's story. It was pretty ugly. Sharon had never known Kris well, though she'd always thought there was something fake about her. But she was stunned to hear the extent to which Kris would go to get what she wanted. On the other hand, it was easy to see why Jade, with her obvious dislike for Greenwood's straight culture, would go along with Kris's plan.

But Sharon wasn't about to cut Jade any slack for this. She knew she should be kind, and try to understand Jade's anger. But Sharon had her own anger. And she let it loose.

"That's really cool, Jade," she said bitterly. "Spreading gossip, hurting someone you don't even know, just to get back at people who never did anything to you. Congratulations. You must be very proud of yourself."

Jade was silent. But now that lower lip was definitely trembling. She mumbled something Sharon couldn't hear.

"What?"

"I said no, I'm not proud of myself."

Sharon waited, but that seemed to be all Jade had to say. Sharon spoke more gently. "Look, Jade, I don't know anything about you. But you don't know anything about me either, or about any of us here. When you're ready to talk . . . I'll be ready to listen. If you'll do the same."

It was painful, watching Jade go even paler than usual. Sharon was glad when she heard footsteps behind her. She turned, expecting to see Debra.

"Hi, Sharon."

"Paula! What are you doing here so late?"

"I had a meeting with the guidance counselor. I just wanted to tell you, I've still got the gown."

"You didn't bring it back to the store?"

Paula smiled ruefully. "They wouldn't take it back. It was on sale."

"Well, maybe you can save it for the senior prom," Sharon suggested.

"I don't think it will fit by then," Paula said dryly.

Sharon was embarrassed. "Sorry. For a moment, I almost forgot."

"That's okay. I wish everyone else would." She glanced curiously at Jade, and Sharon remembered her manners.

"Paula Skinner, Jade Barrow."

Paula smiled and said, "Hi, Jade." Jade didn't say anything. She was staring at Paula with a sort of sick fascination.

"We're talking about the gown Paula bought for homecoming," Sharon said pointedly. "I was hoping she might still be able to wear it."

"It doesn't look promising," Paula said. "Well, I'll see you later. Nice to have met you, Jade."

"Wait," Jade said suddenly. "Could I talk to you for a minute?"

Paula looked puzzled, but she nodded. "Sure."

Sharon wondered if Jade was planning to confess her deed to Paula, and why. But now Debra was coming toward her, so she waved to Paula and Jade and went to meet Debra. As they turned the corner to the school doors, Debra said, "Aren't you going to check the survey box?"

"What's the point?" Sharon asked.

But Debra went to the table where the box had been sitting, and peered inside. "Hey, come look!"

Sharon joined her. There was a pile of folded sheets in the box.

"I've got room in my back pack," Debra said, and she began stuffing the surveys in. "We can go back to your place and look at them."

"Yeah, okay."

"Aren't you pleased to get all these responses?" Debra asked her.

"Why should I be?" Sharon replied. "We both know what they're going to say. Deb . . ."

"What?"

"Do you think I'm a freak, for not making love with Tyler?"

"No," Debra said firmly. "But you're asking the wrong person. I don't even *date.*"

When they arrived at Sharon's house, they

184

went directly to her bedroom. "There's got to be at least fifty here," Debra noted as she spread the surveys out on Sharon's bed. She picked one at random.

"Oh, somebody's trying to be cute. For 'sex', there's a question mark. And for, 'how old were you when you first had sexual relations,' this clown wrote, 'I can't remember back that far.' "

"Ha ha," Sharon commented. "I'll bet they're all going to be like that."

Debra selected another one and started to read.

"Another comedian?" Sharon asked.

"No. Listen to this. 'I was fifteen when I first had sex. I wish I hadn't done it. Once you go all the way, you can't go back."

"Are you making that up?" Sharon asked.

"No. And there's more."

"Let me see that." She took the survey from Debra. As she read, her eyes widened.

Debra had another survey in her hands. "And get this. 'I've never had sex, but I tell people I have.' "

Twenty minutes later, after reading fifty-three surveys, Debra was shaking her head in amazement. "I think we'd better work on your talk for the show. This sort of changes everything, doesn't it?"

In a daze, Sharon didn't respond.

"What are you thinking?" Debra asked.

"I'm thinking . . ." Sharon said slowly, "that maybe I'm not such a freak."

Thirteen

"Sharon, did you get any sleep at all last night?" Mr. Delaney wanted to know at the breakfast table.

Sharon focused bleary eyes on him. "I'm not sure." That was almost true. Even her dreams the night before seemed to involve reciting her newly revised speech. Some of those dreams were nightmares.

"Is that what you're going to wear?" her mother asked with just a hint of criticism in her voice. "What about your new dress, the one with the pretty collar?"

"No, Jeff said we should look ordinary." She brushed a bit of lint off the long green and blue tunic that hung over the blue leggings. *Yes,* she thought, *this is definitely ordinary.* But she'd be comfortable. At least, *physically* comfortable. Her mental state was a disaster.

"What time are you going to be on TV?" Kyle asked.

"We're taping the show at two, and it goes on the air at five."

"Oh, too bad," Kyle remarked. "I'll miss it."

Mrs. Delaney raised her eyebrows. "Why?"

"Same time as 'Gilligan's Island.' "

Mr. Delaney spoke sternly. "I think you can pass up a twenty-year-old rerun to watch your sister."

"I don't know," Mrs. Delaney mused. "Sharon, what do you think? Is the, um, subject matter appropriate for someone Kyle's age?"

Sharon gazed at her brother thoughtfully. In just a few years, he'd be dealing with these problems and hang-ups and pressures-too. He could even turn out to be another Tyler. "I think you should let him watch it."

"Swell," Kyle muttered.

"And be sure to tape it for me," Mr. Delaney ordered.

Sharon shivered. She hadn't even thought about the fact that her own parents would hear her discussing sex on TV. She rose. "I've gotta run. I still have to pass out tickets."

"But you haven't even touched your breakfast," her mother objected.

"Sorry, Mom. But I don't think my stomach's in any condition for food."

"Butterflies, huh?" her father remarked.

"Yeah, a little."

Kyle looked up. "I knew this guy at school who was in a play. He got stage fright and forgot all his lines."

"Thanks a lot," Sharon said. "See ya."

"Break a leg!" her father called after her.

It was a silly show biz expression, Sharon

187

thought. But all the way to school, her legs were so wobbly they *felt* broken. She didn't know how she was going to get through this day.

But somehow, she did. It was easy getting rid of the tickets. Most students would go to anything to get out of a class.

As for her own classes, she put her brain on automatic and drifted from room to room in a fog. Lunch was impossible. Kids kept coming up to her, asking about the show and wishing her luck. They meant well, but it was only making her more nervous. She managed to down half a carton of yogurt before she gave up.

At precisely one o'clock, clutching her notes in a sweaty palm, she went to the studio. The quiet of yesterday was gone. Today, an hour before showtime, the place was a madhouse.

People she didn't recognize scurried about, positioning cameras and adjusting lights. Jeff was talking to one of them when he spotted Sharon and beckoned to her.

"These are the folks from Channel 42," he told her hurriedly. "How are you feeling? Nervous?"

"I'm fine," Sharon lied. "But I've made some changes in the direction of my talk—"

Jeff was distracted by some man who was calling to him."Good, good. Why don't you go get into makeup."

"Makeup?" Sharon asked in mild alarm. "I didn't bring any makeup."

"It's a special treat for the first show. The TV station sent over a professional makeup artist. She's in the storage room."

188

He waved her toward the exit at the opposite side of the studio, and he took off to consult with one of the camera men.

Sharon went out of the studio and crossed the corridor to the storage room. Tyler was coming out.

He looked distinctly uncomfortable, and Sharon knew why. His face was unnaturally polished with a pinkish glow. Involuntarily Sharon grinned.

Tyler did, too. Then, as if they both remembered at the very same moment, the smiles disappeared. She passed by him and went into the storage room.

A woman in a white lab coat was busily slapping powder on Kris, who was wrapped in a white sheet. Kris spoke to Sharon's reflection in the mirror. "Hi, Sharon! Isn't this fun? I've never had my makeup done professionally before."

"Hi, Kris." It was hard looking Kris in the face, knowing what she'd done to Paula.

"I'll be with you in just a second," the woman told Sharon. "I'm almost finished." She whipped the sheet off Kris.

Sharon could see that Kris hadn't taken Jeff's advice on clothes. She was all dressed up in a gauzy dress. "See you later!" she chirped as she walked out.

Sharon took her place, and the makeup artist scrutinized her face.

"Pretty hopeless, huh?" Sharon said.

"Not at all. I'm going to give you cheekbones."

"Can I keep them?" Sharon joked weakly.

The woman went to work. Sharon actually found it relaxing to sit there, with eyes closed, feeling the woman's gentle touch. She was almost sorry when it was over.

But then the other homecoming candidates streamed in, and the room was immediately filled with the sounds of giggles and animated chatter. Sharon was glad she could escape.

She met Jade just outside the room. Jade *had* taken Jeff's advice—she looked just like she always did. With one addition. "You've got a tattoo!" Sharon exclaimed.

Jade turned slightly so Sharon could get a better view of the deep red heart stabbed by a dagger on her upper arm. "Pretty cool, huh?" Her expression challenged Sharon to disagree.

"Didn't it hurt?"

"No big deal." Her eyes were darting about, as if she was looking for someone.

"Are you nervous?" Sharon asked.

"No!" Jade snapped, with an intensity that made Sharon hold up her hands to ward off possible blows.

"Okay, okay, I was just asking." Sharon turned away.

"Sharon?"

She looked back.

"Yeah, I'm nervous," Jade confessed. "You?"

"Can't you hear my teeth chattering?"

Jeff came out of the studio. "Sharon, Jade . . . let's get the whole group together."

A moment later they were all assembled. Sharon scanned the group and recognized tension among them all. Zack's lips were pressed together in a tight line. Tyler leaned against the wall with his eyes closed.

Only Debra seemed completely relaxed. But as the only one who wouldn't be on camera, she could afford to be calm.

Jeff was trying to sound calm, but he wasn't having much success. "Okay, guys, this is it. Our first show. Now, nobody's expecting perfection, but I want to see some sparks. This is your chance to show the world what's really going on with young people. Don't hold back. Let it all out."

Sharon wondered if anyone else was listening to this pep talk. Her own head was too cluttered to absorb much more than every other word. Plus, there was a distracting noise, a sort of rumbling which seemed to be coming from behind the door leading into the studio.

She edged a few steps backward and peeked through the glass window in the door. Her heart skipped a beat. The bleachers that faced the stage were almost filled. More students were filing in. They had an audience.

In a futile attempt to erase the image of the crowd from her mind, she concentrated on Jeff's final words.

"So get out there and do your best. And don't be afraid to show your real feelings. That's the only way to get others to show theirs."

She was seized by panic. Real feelings . . . . Did she really expect the apathetic, too-cool-for-words students at Greenwood High to expose real feelings? But there was no time to dwell on that. This was what she'd always wanted—an opportunity to explore real problems, significant issues. This was her big chance and she wasn't going to blow it.

"What did Jeff say about the changes?" Debra whispered in her ear.

"He doesn't know. There wasn't time to tell him."

And then Jeff touched her arm. "It's time."

She willed her legs to move. Somehow, she found herself on the stage, taking a seat. Zack was in the seat next to her, and Tyler was at the podium on the edge of the stage.

Blinded by the bright lights, she couldn't see the audience, and she hoped that condition would continue. It would be a lot easier saying what she wanted to say without having to *see* them. And Tyler, at the podium, was out of her range of vision, too. She was grateful for that. She didn't even want to consider how he might respond.

She could hear Jeff asking the audience to be quiet, and then asking if the group on stage were ready. Her head went up and down. Then he called, "Action!"

Tyler began speaking. "Good afternoon, and welcome to the first edition of 'Video High.' Today, we'll be addressing two topics. First, we're going to discuss the current controversy regarding whether or not condoms should be distributed in high schools. Later, we'll be talking with the candidates for this year's homecoming queen."

Sharon marveled at how cool and confident he

sounded. She let her eyes drift toward him. No wonder he was speaking so smoothly. He had his notecards right on the podium.

Her eyes were becoming accustomed to the lights, and she could make out some faces now. She kept her eyes on Debra, who gave her a thumbs-up gesture.

"Our first speaker," Tyler continued, "will be—damn!"

"Cut!" Jeff yelled. "What's the problem?"

"I dropped the cards," Tyler said. He was gathering them up from the floor. People in the audience tittered, and Sharon's heart went out to him. He had to be so embarrassed.

"Ready?" Jeff asked. "Okay, action!"

"The first speaker is Zack Stevenson, who will present the case against condom distribution."

Sharon hoped her gasp wasn't audible. She realized that Tyler must have mixed up the cards, and she stole a glance at Zack. He, too, looked flustered, but he recovered quickly.

"Schools have no business becoming involved in the private lives of students," he began. What followed were the same arguments Sharon had heard at the school board meeting. It wasn't easy keeping her features arranged in an expression of polite interest when she wanted to yawn.

"Condoms only encourage students to engage in sexual activities." As Zack droned on in a monotone, Sharon began to examine the audience. No one was yawning or rolling eyes, but they didn't seem to be particularly fascinated, either. Most of them looked bored.

I won't bore them, Sharon thought. They might be surprised, or upset, or even shocked, but they're not going to be bored. And with that encouraging mental pep talk, she was ready when Zack finished.

Tyler had managed to find the right card, and he introduced her properly. She took a deep breath and began.

"We all know about the threat of AIDS, and we know that AIDS is spreading among teenage populations. We know that the best way to protect yourself from AIDS is by using condoms. So, it's obvious that we need to have condoms made easily available so that we can protect ourselves from contacting the AIDS virus through sexual relations."

She paused, and surveyed the audience. They were just as bored as they'd been when Zack was speaking. But she'd expected that. Now she was going to wake them up.

"I'm not going to give a lecture about it here. You know the facts about AIDS, and the facts about condoms. We've all received pamphlets about it, we hear about it on TV, we read about it everywhere. But what about sexual relations? Do you understand what *that's* all about?"

Someone in the audience yelled something, but Sharon couldn't make it out. Luckily, Tyler remembered his job. He leaped off the stage with his microphone, ran up the bleachers, and located the student.

Sharon couldn't see the speaker but she could hear him well enough.

"No, we don't understand what it's all about. Tell us how to do it, Sharon!"

"Very funny," Sharon retorted. "Seriously, guys, this is important and it's something worth talking about. Of course, people *do* talk about it, all the time. They brag about it. They make jokes about it. And everyone knows *how* to have sex. But what no one wants to talk about is *why* they're having sex."

"Because it feels good," someone yelled, loud enough to be heard without the microphone.

Sharon didn't wait for the giggles to die down. "There's more to it than that and you know it," she declared loudly. "There are other reasons people have sex. Let's talk about them."

She could sense the audience stirring, sitting up straighter, paying attention. And she tried not to think about the fact that Tyler was out there, too, watching and listening. Luckily, he was standing in a shadow, and she couldn't see his reaction.

"Here are some of the reasons I've been hearing," she went on. "Some kids have sex because of peer pressure. Their friends are having sex, or at least, they *say* they're having sex, so they have to do it, too—even if they're not in love or committed to anyone.

"There are guys who push a girl to have sex because they think it's expected of them. There are girls who go along because they're afraid they'll lose their boyfriends if they don't. Kids who don't want it and who're not ready for it are having sex. Why are people doing this? What do you think?"

Her question was greeted with dead silence.

She kept her rising panic under control. They were probably embarrassed, too chicken to speak up. They'd needed some coaxing. She pressed on. "I know you've got feelings about this. I've read the surveys you returned. C'mon, let's hear them."

But still, there was nothing. Then, Tyler stepped out from a shadow, and she could see him clearly. There was something in his face, something she couldn't read at first . . . and then, she began to understand.

"We're scared, aren't we?" she asked, more softly. "We're confused and scared and no one wants to talk about it, no one knows how anyone else is really feeling. We think we're alone. So we do things we might not be ready to do, because we don't know what else to do. Right?"

She screamed silently, *please, someone, speak. say something, say anything.* She knew if she could get one person talking, others would follow. Then, her stomach did a flip-flop. Mr. Quimby was standing by the door. She hoped the kids in the audience didn't see him. She'd never get them to talk with him in the room.

Way, way, in the back, she could see a hand slowly rising. Tyler saw it, too. He began to make his way up the bleachers. This is it, Sharon thought. It's going to happen.

Tyler was edging down the row. He reached the girl. "Do you have an opinion on this?"

The girl spoke haltingly. "I think some people jump into having sex because—"

"Stop! Stop this at once!"

The familiar bark came from the entrance.

"Cut!" Jeff yelled.

Mr. Quimby strode to the center of the room. Jeff hurried forward to meet him.

"This is outrageous!" the assistant principal fumed. "I won't have this program turned into some sort of teenage sex fantasy." His eyes were practically bulging out of his head. "This is exactly the sort of thing I was worried about. I will *not* have all of Atlanta thinking Greenwood is a school of sex maniacs!" He shot a fierce glare at Sharon, who shrank back in her seat.

"Have you got anything else planned for this show?" he asked Jeff.

"The interview with homecoming queen candidates," Jeff told him.

"Then get on to that."

Jeff started to protest, but Quimby cut him off. He lowered his voice so the audience couldn't hear him, but Sharon could make out the words. "You do what I say or this whole project is cancelled. Understand?"

Zack jumped off the stage and proceeded to shake Mr. Quimby's hand. "Thank you, sir. This was becoming a major embarrassment."

Jeff turned to Sharon and gave her a hopeless, helpless shrug. With as much dignity as she could muster, she rose and left the stage.

Fourteen

Sharon's face burned as she sidled along the wall of the studio. The last time she could remember feeling this way was back in third grade, when a teacher had ordered her out of the room for passing a note. That same sense of public humiliation was with her now. Fiercely, she fought back tears.

Debra edged over next to her and briefly squeezed her hand.

"Quimby's an ass and everyone knows that," she whispered. "Look, he's leaving."

Sharon pulled herself together. "I guess he figures homecoming queens won't say anything shocking."

Jeff clapped his hands and the buzz of the audience died down. "Okay, folks, we're going to resume. Tyler?"

Tyler returned to the podium. A few giggles could be heard as Jade made her way onto the stage. Sharon had to admire the way Jade ignored the audience reaction to her appearance. At the same time, she was apprehensive. The show certainly hadn't gone very well so far, and she seriously doubted that Jade would make much effort to improve the situation.

She sat down and adjusted the microphone. "Action," Jeff called. Tyler was subdued as he introduced Jade.

To Sharon's surprise, neither Jade's expression nor her tone of voice communicated belligerence. "Tomorrow, the students here at Greenwood will vote for this year's homecoming queen, who will be crowned at half-time during Saturday night's football game. Students all over Atlanta and the rest of the country are doing the same this season. But what do we really know about the girls we crown? What qualifications does a girl need to be an effective homecoming queen? On what basis will you cast your vote?"

Sharon had to press her lips together to keep from laughing, and Debra covered her mouth to hide her smile. Jade's serious tone and solemn demeanor suggested that she was about to present the candidates for U.S. president, not homecoming queen. Sharon suspected she was doing this on purpose. It was her way of mocking the whole business.

She introduced Dana Baldwin first, who pranced onto the set as if she appeared on TV everyday. Jade didn't bother with any small talk. "Dana, why do you want to be homecoming queen?"

Dana was prepared for that. She beamed at Jade. "What girl wouldn't? It's a great honor."

"Why?"

Dana was clearly caught off guard. "What do you mean, why?"

"Why would you consider being crowned at half-time in a football game an honor?"

"Well, because . . . because it means the students think I'd be a good representative."

Jade nodded slowly. "I see. Is that what a homecoming queen should be? A representative of the student body?"

"Yes."

"Then it seems to me the homecoming queen should be someone typical, average. Ordinary. Is that how you see yourself? Ordinary? Sort of a run-of-the-mill student?"

Dana was floundering. "Well, I think students would want someone special to represent them . . ."

Jade pounced on that. "So you think you're special. What makes you so special, Dana?"

Sharon could imagine what was going on in the girl's head. Should she deny being special? Should she start bragging and run the risk of coming across as a show-off?

Dana stammered a few remarks about her school activities, her commitment to Greenwood and her love of every single student that walked the hallways. When she paused to take a breath, Jade broke in.

"That's very interesting, Dana, and thank you very much for joining us on 'Video High.'"

From where Sharon was standing, she could see Jeff frowning and trying to signal something to Jade. Debra saw this, too. "She's going too fast."

Sharon checked her watch. The show still had forty-five minutes to run. Jade would never fill that much time if all the interviews were this brief.

But if Jade was aware of this, she gave no indication. She ignored Jeff's signals, and introduced the next candidate. And she conducted her next two interviews at the same speed, hitting the candidates with a barrage of rapid questions but interrupting them if they went on too long with their answers.

"Why is she doing this?" Debra asked.

"I don't know," Sharon replied. But Jade wasn't stupid. If she was rushing the interviews, she had to have her reason.

Behind the stage, waiting to make her entrance, Kris was wondering the same thing. As Jade sped through the interviews, she became nervous. Was Jade reserving extra time for *her*? And if so . . . why?

She didn't let herself ponder this for long. I've got nothing to worry about, she told herself. Anything Jade accuses me of doing, I'll just deny. No one's going to believe her, anyway.

Jade was introducing her. Kris strode out onto the stage, prepared for battle. Jade actually cracked a smile for her, which didn't ease Kris's nerves at all. If anything, it put her guard up even more.

"Welcome to 'Video High,' Kris. And congratulations on your last-minute candidacy."

Was it her imagination, or was Jade stressing the words 'last minute?'" Thank you, Jade. It certainly came as a complete surprise to me."

Jade arched her eyebrows. "Oh, really?" she said, with just a hint of exaggeration.

"Yes, really," Kris replied smoothly. No way was she going to let this geek throw her off balance.

"Tell me, Kris, do you think you have a chance at the crown?"

"Oh, gosh, I don't know, Jade. I suppose students will vote for the girl who they think best represents Greenwood. And it would be wonderful if that girl was me! But it doesn't matter if I'm chosen or not. It's a thrill simply to have been nominated."

"Even if you were just a last-minute substitute?" Jade murmured.

Kris could feel the strain in her own smile, but she kept it firmly in place. "It's still an honor."

"Of course it is," Jade said. "Kris, what makes you qualified to be homecoming queen?"

Kris brightened. This was the kind of question she'd prepared for. She plunged into a lively description of her activities, her commitment to Greenwood High, and her love of football.

"I was a cheerleader, so I've been to every football game at Greenwood. Since my accident, I haven't been on the squad, but I wouldn't miss a game. So many girls have no real interest in football. They don't even know anything about how the game is played. I think it's very important

202

for a homecoming queen to have a real love for and understanding of football."

She was so wrapped up in her speech that she didn't notice the little gleam in Jade's eyes until she had finished. Jade's next question was unexpected.

"So, you are one of the few girls here who's a real authority on football. Could you take a few minutes and explain the game to the rest of us ignorant females?"

Kris tried to still the panic rising inside her. "Oh, I wouldn't want to bore everyone."

"Go right ahead, Kris. Bore us."

Only the audience and the cameras kept Kris from showing her panic. Or slapping Jade's smug face. Fortunately, fury fueled her brain.

"I'd rather not, Jade. I don't think it's fair to the other candidates for me to show off my knowledge of football." She stood up. "And I've already taken up more air time than they had. Thank you, Jade." She paused to smile brightly, first at the audience, then at the camera.

"Cut!" Jeff called out.

Kris turned and glared at Jade. She wanted to wipe off that smile with a slap, but there was an audience watching. As she left the stage, she comforted herself. Okay, maybe Jade had made her look a little foolish. But it could have been worse. A lot worse.

In a way, she'd gotten off easy.

* * *

"We've still got almost forty minutes to fill," Sharon said.

Debra nodded. "I know. This is a nightmare."

The audience was getting restless as Jeff conferred with Jade. Sharon couldn't hear them, but she could see that Jade was speaking rapidly. Jeff was rubbing his forehead and frowning. Finally, he nodded, and Jade returned to her seat on the stage.

"Action!"

"Our last interview today is with a girl who *was* a homecoming queen candidate. I'd like to introduce Paula Skinner."

A buzz went through the audience. Debra turned to Sharon. "What's going on?"

"I don't have the slightest idea," Sharon replied, watching Paula walk onto the stage. What was Jade up to?

"Paula, you were a candidate for homecoming queen," Jade began. "And now you're not. Why is that? Did you drop out of the running?"

"No," Paula replied. "I was informed by a member of the school administration that I could no longer be a candidate."

"What reason were you given?"

"Because I'm pregnant."

Sharon gazed out at the audience. Many of the kids looked stunned. Most of them probably already knew about Paula, but hearing her announce it publicly was a shock.

"Why would being pregnant make you ineligible to be homecoming queen?"

"I don't know," Paula said. "But I suppose the

administration thinks I'd present a bad example for the students. Being pregnant means I've had sexual relations. They think that if a homecoming queen, or a candidate, admits to having had sex, other kids might be encouraged to have sex."

"Do you think they need encouragement?" Jade asked.

Paula smiled. "No."

Debra whispered in Sharon's ear. "Jade's really *good* at this!"

Sharon shared Debra's impression. Jade sounded just like a real television personality.

Jade turned to the audience. "What do you think? Did the administration do the right thing in dumping Paula? Is it wrong to admit that high school students are having sex?"

Sharon could see Tyler searching the audience for any sign of response. There wasn't any. But Tyler went directly to a boy sitting on the aisle, and spoke into the microphone.

"Do you think it's wrong for high school students to have sex?" he asked bluntly. Then he stuck the mike into the boy's face.

Sharon gasped. That wasn't exactly Jade's question. And Tyler had spoken as if he, personally, wanted an answer.

"Hell, no," the boy muttered, looking embarrassed.

Tyler moved to the girl sitting next to him. "What about you? Do you think it's wrong to have sex?"

The girl's face turned red. "It's not wrong, exactly . . ." She pushed the mike away, but everyone could hear her say, I don't want to talk about this."

"Why?" Jade asked from the stage. "Is having sex something to be ashamed of?"

A hand in the first row went up. Tyler started down the steps. At the same time, two girls in the back raised their hands. Suddenly, Jeff shoved a microphone into Sharon's hands. "Go help him out."

Sharon ran up to the last row. Along the way, she heard the boy up front speaking. "I'm not ashamed. But sex is something private."

Sharon extended her microphone to one of the girls in the back. "If it's so private, then why do kids talk about doing it all the time?"

The girl next to her spoke. "They don't talk about it, they *joke* about it. And half of them are lying anyway."

"Why do they lie?" Sharon asked.

"I don't know."

But half a dozen other students had an opinion. Sharon and Tyler raced around the audience to get their comments.

"I know why kids lie. Because they want to be cool."

"Because everyone else is doing it and you don't want to look like a wimp."

Hands were flying, and some kids weren't even waiting for the microphone.

"People act like it's no big deal, as long as you don't get a disease. Or pregnant."

"Yeah, but there are other things to think about, too. Like, whether you're having sex because you want to or because you think you're supposed to."

"Sex should be special. It's not just shaking hands."

"Some guys *expect* you to do it with them."

"Some girls expect it, too!"

Sharon approached a girl who was shaking her head. "What's your opinion?"

"There are kids who are having sex who shouldn't be," the girl said.

"Why?" Sharon asked. "Because it's wrong? Because they're too young?"

"No," the girl said. "Because they're doing it for the wrong reasons."

The boy next to her agreed. "And some people just aren't ready."

Sharon moved on to another girl. "What do you do when a guy wants to have sex with you?" she asked.

The girl shrugged. "If I like him a lot . . . I guess I might. But I might not. It depends . . ."

"On what?"

"On if it feels right."

"What if a guy puts a lot of pressure on you to have sex?" Sharon asked another girl.

"I might give in."

"Even if you don't really want to do it?"

Silently, the girl nodded.

Sharon turned to move on down the aisle and bumped right into Tyler. They stared at each other for a moment, and then Tyler looked away and spoke into his microphone. "How would you feel if a girl you like refused to have sex with you?" He held the mike in front of a boy.

"I'd feel like she doesn't really care about me."

Sharon spoke into her own mike. "Maybe she cares about you but she's not ready for such a big step. Did you ever think of that?"

Tyler spoke into *his* mike. "Sex is what people do when they care about each other."

"Is that some law I've never heard of?" Sharon asked.

"Can I say something?" Jade called out.

Sharon had almost forgotten about Jade and Paula, still sitting on the stage. She forced her angry eyes away from Tyler and gave Jade her attention.

"It seems to me," Jade said, "that a lot of you are having sex, or thinking about having it. You don't need any encouragement at all. So why shouldn't the administration let Paula be a homecoming queen candidate?"

Sharon thought she had the answer to that. "They don't want Paula to be a homecoming queen for the same reason they don't want condoms in the school. They don't really *care* if we're having sex, as long as it doesn't show. They just want it kept secret, not out in the open. They don't want to talk about it, and they don't want to acknowledge that we have feelings about it."

Jade turned to the camera. "I think we've opened up a new dialogue here on 'Video High'. I'd like to see this kind of discussion continue." She turned to her guest. "And I'd like to see

208

Paula on the football field at half-time Saturday night. What do the rest of you think?"

The applause began slowly, then rose to a crescendo. The camera panned the audience.

And Jeff, with his first real smile of the day, yelled "Cut!"

Fifteen

On Friday morning, when she entered school, Sharon learned what it meant to be a celebrity. She'd become one, overnight.

Surrounded by fans, she was speechless. "Sharon!" Lori squealed. "Your show was fantastic!"

"Fabulous!" Beth Ann echoed.

Sandra was giggling. "You know, I only watched to see Zack Stevenson. He's so excellent! But when you started talking to everyone in the audience, I was hooked!"

Sharon could barely squeeze a "thanks" into the conversation. "And the girl who interviewed Paula was unbelievable," Lori said. "Who was she?"

"Jade Barrow," Sharon said, but she didn't think anyone could hear her. Beth Ann was asking, "Can people still sign up to work on the show?"

"We're having a meeting today, after school."

On her way to her homeroom, she was stopped every few seconds by students telling her how much they liked "Video High" and several asked about working on the next show. Sharon told them about the meeting, but mentally she added, *if there is a next show.* She had a pretty good idea what Mr. Quimby's reaction must have been to it. For all she knew, "Video High" may already have been canceled.

But she couldn't worry about that now. All she wanted to do was revel in the joy of a big success. "Jade! Wait up!"

Jade turned. "What do you want?"

Sharon stopped short. There it was again—the old hostility. Confused, Sharon stammered, "I didn't get to talk to you after the show yesterday. You disappeared the second we finished taping."

Jade's eyes narrowed. "What did you want to talk to me about?" she asked suspiciously.

"I just wanted to thank you. For getting Paula onto the show."

Jade's suspicion was replaced by uncertainty. "You're not angry?"

"Why would I be angry?" Then it hit her. "You mean, because you got the audience to talk and I couldn't?"

Dumbly, Jade nodded.

Sharon shook her head in exasperation. "Jade, we're all in this together. It's not a competition, for crying out loud. I'm just glad *somebody* pulled it off."

"Really?"

"Absolutely. The show was a hit. That's all that matters. And you were outstanding! Everyone's talking about you."

Jade's lips twitched. "They were doing that before I ever went on TV."

When she walked into her homeroom, Sharon was once again engulfed in praise and congratulations from the other students. Debra got a lot of attention, too—even though she hadn't appeared on the screen, lots of kids had noticed her name in the credits at the end.

Sharon was almost glad when the bell rang, and everyone had to settle down. She wanted a few quiet moments, to relive the triumph of "Video High."

She'd watched the program with her brother. Her mother had been delayed at a faculty meeting, and her father had been at work, too. She could still feel the trepidation she'd experienced as she put a blank tape into the VCR, and hit record on the remote.

Within a few minutes, her apprehension had eased. It was amazing, the way Jeff and the TV people had edited the program in just a few hours. It flowed so smoothly that no one could have been aware of all the interruptions that took place during the actual taping. There were funny moments, like when a close-up caught Kris's panic as Jade asked her to explain football. And another close-up created a poignant moment when it caught a tear in Paula's eyes.

But the real excitement came when the cameras captured the intensity and enthusiasm of the audience. When the show was over, Kyle turned to her.

"Cool."

It was the highest praise she could have hoped to receive from him. And she knew that she, along with the entire "Video High" crew, deserved it. Something important had just happened, and she'd been part of making it happen.

When her parents came home, she'd watched the tape of the show with them. She took their praise with a grain of salt—as her parents, they *had* to like it. But their compliments were confirmed as the phone started ringing. Talking to the friends who called, Sharon got a real sense of the show's impact.

Her reverie was broken when a messenger appeared in class with a note for the teacher.

"Sharon, Debra, you're wanted in the assistant principal's office."

The girls exchanged resigned looks. As they walked the silent hall, Sharon fought to retain some optimism. "Mr. Quimby isn't stupid. He's got to realize the show was a success."

"Was," Debra echoed. "Past tense." She sighed. "I finally find an extracurricular activity that isn't boring or trivial, and it's killed off."

The secretary looked up from the newspaper she was reading when they walked in. "We're supposed to see Mr. Quimby," Sharon told her.

"He's on the phone. Have a seat."

Jade came in. She sighed in relief when she saw Sharon and Debra. "Oh, good. I thought it was just me he's after."

Tyler came in, nodded at the others and slumped down in a chair. He was followed by Zack, the only one who didn't look depressed.

"Well, I hope you're all satisfied," he said to the group, and then addressed Jade in particular. "Especially you. You sabotaged the show with your stupid stunt."

Sharon was enraged. "Are you crazy? She saved the show!"

Debra nodded vigorously, and Tyler was roused from his slump. "Yeah, you're out of your mind, Zack."

"Hold on, you guys," Jade said. "I can defend myself." She turned to Zack. "Blow it out your ear, bozo."

Zack had no opportunity to respond. Jeff walked in. *He* didn't seem upset. "Listen, guys. Whatever happens in there, I'm proud of you."

There was a buzz, and the secretary picked up the phone.

"Yes, sir." To the group, she said, "You can go in now."

"Where's Kris?" Sharon asked.

"Probably campaigning," Debra replied.

"Oh, right." Sharon had completely forgotten that the students were voting today.

They all went into the inner office. Any faint hope Sharon retained for "Video High" evaporated with one look at Quimby's face. His expression said it all, but he had plenty of words for them, too.

"When I saw the name of Greenwood High School associated with that trash yesterday, I was appalled. *Appalled!*"

Zack spoke up. "Sir, I just want to tell you that I personally share your feelings and—"

Quimby cut him off. "Do you realize what kind of image you projected? Do you have any idea what you've done to the reputation of this school? I will not tolerate—What do you want?"

The secretary had come in with her newspaper. "Just thought you might like to see this, Mr. Quimby." She tossed the open newspaper on his desk. As she walked out, Sharon could have sworn she saw her wink at Jeff.

As Mr. Quimby scanned the article, Sharon read the headline upside-down. 'Teen TV Show Worth a Look' it read. Jeff moved alongside the assistant principal, and read aloud.

" 'Video High,' an hour-long show presented by students at Greenwood High School, made an impressive debut yesterday. If the first show is any indication of things to come, te nagers and their parents have something to look forward to. The lively and provocative discussion—"

Quimby closed the newspaper. "That's enough," he snapped.

"Sounds as if they liked it," Tyler said.

The assistant principal shot him a fierce look. "The media always likes trash. It sells papers. Now, as I was saying—" He was interrupted by the door opening again. This time, however, he didn't question the intruder. "Good morning, Dr. Moorhead."

The dignified, gray-haired woman smiled. "Dr. Quimby, Mr. Russell . . ."

Sharon gazed at the woman in awe. The students hardly ever saw the principal except at assemblies, and no one was quite sure what she actually did. Still, she was a highly respected figure.

"Are you the students who were involved in 'Video High?' I was very impressed with your program yesterday. I'll look forward to seeing it every week. Congratulations." She shook hands with each one of them, and left.

Mr. Quimby stared after her. Then his phone buzzed. "I said no calls," he yelled at the secretary. Then his expression changed. "Oh! Put him through." After a moment, he said, "Yes sir, how are you, sir. Oh? Why, yes, he's here in my office now." With an expression of total disbelief, he turned to Jeff. "It's the superintendent of schools."

Jeff took the phone. "Hello, this is Jeff Russell. Thank you, sir. I appreciate that. I'll pass it along to the students." He replaced the receiver. "He says he enjoyed the show, and that we have his support to continue addressing, and I quote, 'these important and significant issues.'"

Sharon almost felt sorry for Mr. Quimby. The man looked like he could explode. Just then, Kris came in. "I'm sorry I'm so late," she said.

"The meeting's over," Quimby said. He pointed a stern finger at them all, and said, "I'll be watching you."

"I hope so," Jeff said smoothly.

In the outer office, the group gathered around Jeff. "Well, we've still got a show," Jeff said. "And we're going to have to get right to work if we're going to begin weekly shows next month."

"We can't start *now*," Kris said. "Everyone has to get to their homerooms to vote."

"I'll see you all after school," Jeff said. The group split up. Sharon, Debra, and Jade walked together.

"I don't want to miss the homecoming queen vote," Jade said.

"Are you joking?" Debra asked. "Who are you going to vote for?"

"I thought I might do a write-in," Jade said casually.

Sharon nodded. "That's not a bad idea."

"Are you going to the game tonight?" Jade asked.

"I haven't decided. I had a date with Tyler, but . . . . I don't suppose you guys would want to go. Aren't you just the least bit curious to see who's crowned?"

Debra sighed. "I'd say no, but you'd only talk me into it. Yeah, okay, I'll go."

"Me, too," Jade said unexpectedly.

Debra looked at her with interest. "You know, Jade, you're full of surprises. I think there may be more to you than meets the eye."

"Or less," Sharon said thoughtfully. She was looking at Jade's arm. "Where's your tattoo?"

Jade grinned. "I washed it off. It was a fake."

"Two Four Six Eight, Who do we appreciate? Greenwood, Greenwood, Yay!"

The chanting of the cheerleaders rang all the way to the back of the bleachers where Sharon

217

sat with Jade and Debra. "Are we winning?" Debra asked. "I can't follow this game at all."

"Too bad we don't have Kris with us to explain it all," Jade said.

Sharon laughed. It felt good being here. She'd worried about seeing Tyler, maybe with another date. She'd been afraid of the pain she knew she would feel. But she was having a great time with Debra and Jade, and it would have been silly to pass up the big event.

"Can you believe how many kids showed up at the meeting yesterday?" Debra said.

"Too many," Sharon said. "We're not even going to get to work on the next show."

"Don't complain about that," Jade advised. "Do you really think you could work at that pace every week? Hey, what's happening now?"

"It's half-time," Sharon told her.

They watched the majorettes and the drill team perform, and listened to the school band. A flowered canopy was set up in the middle of the field. Mr. Quimby stood under it.

"It is my pleasure to introduce this year's homecoming court." As he announced Dana, Tracy, Veronica and Kris, each girl was escorted onto the field. Mr. Quimby was handed an envelope by a student.

"The Greenwood High homecoming queen is . . ." He opened the envelope. Even from a distance, Sharon could see him do a double-take. "Paula Skinner?"

A roar went up from the crowd. Sharon cheered and applauded as a startled-looking Paula was pulled down from the bleachers. In blue jeans and a sweatshirt, she made a distinct contrast to the other candidates in their gowns. But she looked beautiful. And very happy.

"There's proof of the power of television!" Jade cried gleefully. "We weren't the only ones to do a write-in vote!"

Now kids were rising, to give the new homecoming queen a standing ovation. That was when Sharon spotted Tyler.

He *was* with a girl, who Sharon didn't recognize. He, too, was applauding and smiling. And the pain Sharon had feared hit her hard.

But she fought it off, and counted her blessings. I'm here, she thought, with an old friend and a new friend, and I'm having a good time. A really nice girl, someone I like, has overcome hypocrisy and is being crowned homecoming queen. Only a few weeks ago, I was bored out of my mind, but I held onto the hope of doing something important, and now I am. "Video High" is going to survive.

She had a lot to be grateful for.

As for Tyler . . . well they'd still be working together. They'd have to see each other. Seeing could lead to talking. Talking could lead to dating. Dating could lead to . . . the same old problem.

Funny, how they were all able to talk about it on television, what they couldn't talk about privately. Well, maybe the show was a beginning.

The power of television . . . . It could change people's minds. If it could change the way a person thought, and felt, then maybe it could help two people understand each other.

The power of television . . . . In the weeks and months to come, and she vowed to find out just how powerful it was.

Look for *Video High #2: The High Life,* coming in April 1994!

And next month, keep an eye out for the first book in another exciting new Z*FAVE series—Z*FAVE'S VOICES OF A GENERATION—A VOICES ROMANCE #1: *Second to None,* by Ar-Lynn Presser.

THE NIGHT OWL CLUB
IT'S COOL—
IT'S FUN—
IT'S TERRIFYING—
AND YOU CAN JOIN IT . . . IF YOU DARE!

THE NIGHTMARE CLUB #1: JOY RIDE   (4315, $3.50)
by Richard Lee Byers

All of Mike's friends know he has a problem—he doesn't see anything wrong with drinking and driving. But then a pretty new girl named Joy comes to The Night Owl Club, and she doesn't mind if he drinks and drives. In fact, she encourages it. And what Mike doesn't know might kill him because Joy is going to take him on the ride of his life!

THE NIGHTMARE CLUB #2: THE INITIATION   (4316, $3.50)
by Nick Baron

Kimberly will do anything to join the hottest clique at her school. And when her boyfriend, Griff, objects to her new "bad" image, Kimberly decides that he is a wimp. Then kids start drowning in a nearby lake—and she starts having nightmares about an evil water spirit that has a hold over her new friends. Kimberly knows that she must resist the monster's horrible demands in order to save Griff and the other kids' lives—and her very soul!

THE NIGHTMARE CLUB #3: WARLOCK GAMES   (4317, $3.50)
by Richard Lee Byers

Mark, the newest cadet at Hudson Military Academy, is falling for Laurie, a student at rival school, Cooper High. So, he does not want to be involved in the feud between the two schools. But fellow cadet, Greg Tobias, persuades Mark to join other cadets in playing weird and violent pranks on Cooper High. Then Mark discovers that Greg is a centuries-old warlock who is playing a deadly game of chess with a fellow demon in which the students are the pawns—and now Mark must break Greg's deadly hold or they will all become victims of a terrifying evil . . .

THE NIGHTMARE CLUB #4: THE MASK   (4349, $3.50)
by Nick Baron

While looking for a costume for the Nightmare Club's Halloween party, average-looking Sheila finds a weird mask in a local antique barn. When she puts it on, she turns into a real knockout, and soon is getting lots of attention. Then good-looking kids start dying and Sheila realizes the truth. When she wears the mask, its guardian spirit gets stronger. And unless Sheila can resist its seductive magic she will become a prisoner of its murderous evil forever!

WHO DUNNIT? JUST TRY AND FIGURE IT OUT!

THE MYSTERIES OF MARY ROBERTS RINEHART

THE AFTER HOUSE	(2821-0, $3.50/$4.50)
THE ALBUM	(2334-0, $3.50/$4.50)
ALIBI FOR ISRAEL AND OTHER STORIES	(2764-8, $3.50/$4.50)
THE BAT	(2627-7, $3.50/$4.50)
THE CASE OF JENNIE BRICE	(2193-3, $2.95/$3.95)
THE CIRCULAR STAIRCASE	(3528-4, $3.95/$4.95)
THE CONFESSION AND SIGHT UNSEEN	(2707-9, $3.50/$4.50)
THE DOOR	(1895-5, $3.50/$4.50)
EPISODE OF THE WANDERING KNIFE	(2874-1, $3.50/$4.50)
THE FRIGHTENED WIFE	(3494-6, $3.95/$4.95)
THE GREAT MISTAKE	(2122-4, $3.50/$4.50)
THE HAUNTED LADY	(3680-9, $3.95/$4.95)
A LIGHT IN THE WINDOW	(1952-1, $3.50/$4.50)
LOST ECSTASY	(1791-X, $3.50/$4.50)
THE MAN IN LOWER TEN	(3104-1, $3.50/$4.50)
MISS PINKERTON	(1847-9, $3.50/$4.50)
THE RED LAMP	(2017-1, $3.50/$4.95)
THE STATE V. ELINOR NORTON	(2412-6, $3.50/$4.50)
THE SWIMMING POOL	(3679-5, $3.95/$4.95)
THE WALL	(2560-2, $3.50/$4.50)
THE YELLOW ROOM	(3493-8, $3.95/$4.95)